IT ISN'T FAIR

It isn't Fair

IVY BROOKS

Shielded Quill

Maverick, I miss you.

1

Kallie

My head is pounding from the night before. I slip off my couch to drink a gallon of water. I really should have not drank so much last night.

Holden and I are going to class today.

I quickly take a shower and towel dry my hair. Rushing, I put on jeans and a hoodie, knowing it is freezing outside. I open the sliding glass door to my backyard to let my dog, Maverick, outside. I quickly pour a glass of water before going upstairs to brush my teeth.

I grab my phone and slide it into my back pocket. My phone starts to vibrate.

Holden: Wanna grab coffee before class?

Me: Yeah. Meet in 15 minutes.

Maverick comes back inside and lays down on his blanket. I don't blame him. It's winter in Iowa. I don't want to leave my house either when it's this cold. I say goodbye to him and grab my keys from the table by the front door.

I start my car to back out of the driveway when Holden calls. "Are you leaving yet?"

"Yeah, I'm on my way now," I said.

I drive to our favorite coffee shop, Books and Coffee. I scan the parking lot for Holden's car and park beside him. He looks up from his phone.

"Hey, Kallie!"

"Hey!"

He opens his arms for a hug as I lean into him. I quickly pull away and walk to the front doors. It looks like they just opened for the morning.

"Late morning?" I asked Holden.

"Maybe the snow was too bad."

I stand in line with Holden, waiting to order.

"Sorry, we're late opening. There was more snow than I thought this morning," the barista said.

"It's fine," I smile. I hate when people apologize; it makes me feel weird, like I did something wrong.

I order for Holden and me while he goes to set up the table. I wait for our drinks and walk over to him, careful not to spill anything.

"What's your first class?"

"British Literature. What about you?" I said.

"American Lit."

I watch him sip his coffee as I pull out my laptop.

"I have to work today since I took an extra day off. I have to finish editing the manuscript that was sent to me last week," I tell Holden.

"I have to work today, too. I'm not sure I like this new schedule."

I nod in agreement. The internship as a senior in college is hard. We needed the experience of working at publishing, but I never expected to work more than 40 hours a week.

"It will be good for us. Hopefully, when we graduate, we'll get hired full time."

"I hope so. I love this internship, and I get to work with my best friend. It's like a dream job."

I smile as I take a sip of my coffee. Holden is really my only friend at school who truly knows me. It's easy since I've known him my whole life. What I love most about Holden is the fact that he never judges me. When I bought my house after freshman year, my parents thought I was crazy. They wanted me to use my trust fund to pay for college, not buy a house. Holden understood.

"Kallie?" I look up from my laptop.

"I think we should leave for class."

I close my laptop and grab my things.

"Would you like a coffee for the drive?"
Holden asked.

"Yes."

I watch him order two more coffees for us. It's not a far drive, but I love caffeine. I swear, instead of blood, I have coffee in my veins. I follow him out to our cars. I have to turn on my music before I start driving. I hate listening to the radio. I see Holden laughing as I find the perfect song. I settle on my A Day To Remember play list and put my car in reverse.

The drive to campus is fine. I'm surprised to see no traffic, but then again, Iowa doesn't have traffic like other states. I find a parking spot near the building I need and grab my things out of the car. I hurry to my class and sit down in the middle row. Everyone seems sleepy. I can start to feel the caffeine waking me up. I hear a loud phone notification sound. I scrunch my face, looking around to see who is that loud. I realize it's mine. I pull it out of my bag.

Holden: I regret American Lit.

Me: I bet.

I thought I had my phone on silent. It wasn't. I switch it to vibrate.

Holden: Still working today?

Me: Yes.

I can tell Holden is extra bored since he's texting me during class. Usually, he's the one telling me to focus. I wait patiently for this class to be over. The professor must notice that class time is over since she suddenly stops talking. "Sorry, I am very passionate about British Lit. I can go on for hours," she says. I nod out of respect, gather my things, and head to my internship. I run to my car and throw my things in the backseat. I check the time; I'll be cutting it close since the professor kept going on.

I rush past the receptionist and head for my office. I can barely hear Samantha saying, "Hey Kallie," as I run past her. I turn on my computer and while I wait for it to load, I grab my laptop. I start working on the manuscript. I set my timer for three hours so I can leave work on time.

There is a knock on my door, grabbing my attention away from my work. "Come in."

"Kallie, are you almost done editing?" my boss asks.

"I have about five pages left."

"Alright, when you're done, email it back to me."

I watch him walk out of my small office, closing the door behind him. I shake my head, trying to regain my focus. I edit the last five pages and email them to my boss. I try to look busy before he comes back with another manuscript to read.

Me: Work is boring without you

Holden: I know. I'll be back tomorrow. Samantha has already called asking if I'll be back tomorrow.

I roll my eyes; Holden really should get the hint she likes him. I don't understand how he can be so oblivious.

Me: She's totally into you. Ask her out already.

Holden: No, I can't date anyone I work with.

Me: Technically, you don't work with her.

I place my phone back on my desk. I am beyond ready to go home. I check with my boss before telling him my time was up. He tells me to expect an email tonight with a new manuscript to read. I smile back at him before closing his door behind me. I gather my things from my office, walking past Samantha's desk. I hesitate before speaking.

"You should just ask Holden for coffee," I tell her.

"Are you sure? I've been dropping hints, and it's like he doesn't notice."

"Because he doesn't. He's oblivious to that kind of thing."

I smile at her as I turn on my heels to leave. I rush to my car and place my bag in the passenger seat next to me. I smile to myself. I can't believe I told Samantha to ask Holden out.

I drive home and stop at Coffee and Books. I order a white chocolate mocha and a pup cup for Maverick. He loves those things, so I know he'll be happy when I get home with them.

I am so ready to just relax, class gave me a headache. Reading at my computer all day made it worst and now my eyes are hurting. I open my door to be greeted by Maverick. To my surprise, Holden is sitting on my couch with Maverick. Sometimes, I forget he has a key to my house for emergencies.

"I would have got you coffee if I knew you were here," I said.

"Did you tell Samantha to ask me out for coffee?"

I laugh, "Yes, and you should go," I giggle.

"What do you want for dinner since you're here?"

"Pizza?"

I check the weather on my phone. "We're supposed to get a blizzard tomorrow," I tell Holden.

"I think they'll cancel work and school with how bad it's going to be."

"25 inches of snow."

"That's ridiculous," I mumble.

Holden grabs our plates for our pizza, and I cut massive slices while he finds a movie to watch. I grab the pizza pan and some waters before heading to the couch. I begin to feel sleepy, looking over to see Maverick sleeping on his blanket.

"Are you staying or leaving before the snow comes?" I ask.

"I was about to head out."

I walk Holden to the door. I look at Maverick sleeping. I check the time and the weather. I decide to go to bed early tonight. I walk up the steps to my room, Maverick following behind me. I sit on my bed, looking out the window. The snow is starting to fall. I really like how it looks when the snow is falling in front of the street lamps. I change into my pajamas. I have a hard time falling asleep. I stare at the ceiling for hours. I think about my internship and how I graduate in May. I know it's only January, but May is really close. The thought of graduating without a plan scares me.

Maverick's barking wakes me up. I stumble down the stairs to see why he's barking. I see him sitting next to the glass door, wanting to go out. I let him out and decide to make a pot of coffee. I laugh as Maverick runs into the snow. He loves water and snow.

I pour my coffee into my mug. I really hope the emails and texts coming through about not having to work or go to school today are true. I just do not want to be stuck at the office or school. I guess I could stay at Holden's if we do get snowed in since his apartment is close to campus. Just as I sit down on my couch, the text comes from work. Samantha sent us a mass text, saying the snowstorm is going to be too bad to come to the office, so work from home today. That only leaves school, which wouldn't be the end of the world to skip.

"Hey," I decide to call Holden.

"Did you get the text from Samantha?" Holden asks.

"Yes, that's why I'm calling. Are you going to class today?"

"No, she's here right now. Can I call you later?"

"Oh, I want all the details," I say before hanging up the phone.

Maverick and I have all day to ourselves. I should start my editing, but I also want to go back to sleep. I flip through the channels, waiting for anything to spark my interest. To no surprise, there isn't anything except movies I've already seen. I huff out loud, and Maverick looks at me. It's time to start working.

Maverick's bark breaks my focus. I casually notice a man and a woman looking at the house next to mine. It's been on the market for so long; I'm surprised anyone wants to buy it. I move to the window to get a better look. The man is so gorgeous; I assume that's his wife with him, and she is equally perfect. They motion to my window, and I pull the curtain closed before going outside with Maverick.

Maverick is waiting at the back door, waiting for me to open it before he runs out. I sigh as I open the door. "Hurry up, boy," I tell him. I glance over at the house before going back inside. I hear Maverick barking before I make it to the living room. I let Maverick back inside, rushing away from the door.

Knowing I need to work on the manuscript, I grab my laptop from the table and move to the couch to work. I want to open the curtain to see the couple again, but I still find it weird to think someone is moving into that house.After the previous owner died, it sat empty for years.

"Hey, someone is actually looking at the house next to mine."

"The murder house?" asked Holden

"Yes, that one," I said.

"How is your snow day?"

"Eh, lame, just working mostly. What about yours?"

"Samantha is snowed in here. It's nice, actually."

"You're welcome!"

"Yeah, yeah. Can I call you later?"

"Sure."

I hang up with Holden. I am surprised he is with Samantha since he is so against dating a co-worker. I have to focus now; I need to at least start working. I regain my focus and start reading; finally, I get a manuscript that interests me. One reason I hate my internship is that I read the most random ones picked for me. I realize I left my notes in my car, so I slip on my shoes to get them. I realize the couple is still outside looking at the house. I try my best to slip back inside without them noticing me. I can't help but glance back one more time at them.

The snow is really coming down harder now. My stomach starts to growl, and I look at the time to realize it's dinnertime. I can't decide what I want, so I make pizza rolls—quick and simple. My kitchen is getting darker with each passing hour. I close my laptop and place it on the counter for tomorrow.

I climb up the stairs with Maverick. I close the curtain to my bedroom before changing into my pajamas. My room is always the coldest, I turn on my heated blanket and slip into bed.

2

Nash

My neighbor is really creeping me out. She is probably wondering why I bought this house. "The murder house," everyone calls it. Honestly, I don't even know. There was a murder/suicide about 2 years ago and it sat empty. I always loved this house growing up. To my surprise, she was the one that bought my parents' house after they died 4 years ago.

Four years ago. That seems like a lifetime since then.

Clearly, the neighbor is probably the only person in town that has no idea who I am. I plan on her not finding out. I plan on keeping my distance from her. With her peeking out the window watching us, that almost seems impossible. Maybe I should just go over there and tell her I can see her looking at me. I wonder if the realtor would be offended if I just kissed her or hug so she stop looking out the window.

I rub my hands down my jeans. I shouldn't be taking my anger out on her. Hell, I don't even know her name, much less have anything to be angry about.

3

Kallie

I watch snow fall from my living room window. It was a nice winter until now; The blizzard is supposed to end today. I see the man again from the night before. He has tan skin, a perfect mix of light and dark brown hair; not too tall but not too short. I watch the man slip and fall on a patch of fresh snow and ice. I couldn't help but to laugh. The sound of the man and the box hitting the ground alerted my dog, Maverick, a black lab with a goofy bark. Maverick's barking alerted the man next door. When the man turned his head towards my house, he must have noticed me standing there in my living room window, laughing. When his eyes contacted mine, I immediately jumped out of in front of my window.

I waited for a few seconds to peek around at the window. I watch as the man gathers himself from off the ground. His back is covered with snow. Maverick continues to bark, which catches the man's attention again. I watch him walk towards my house. I am standing in the living room nervous about situation that stood before me. On one hand, the man was gorgeous. On the other hand, there was no way the man did not see me laughing from my living room window. I was still standing there hiding behind my door, when I hear steps coming up my porch. The sound of three loud knocks followed. I got myself together. I did a quick once over in the mirror. My makeup was alright, definitely could use a touch up. My hair scattered to all parts of my scalp and my shirt had a coffee stain from my morning cup.

While I was standing there trying to figure out if I was presentable, I heard the knock again. The knock pulled me out of my head and back into reality. I hesitantly opened the door, before I could say anything, his eyes took my voice away. They are hazel and dreamy. They look like they could talk... I am not sure what I even mean by that.

"Hello, I am Nash."

I stand in the doorway looking dumb founded, completely lost in his eyes.

"Hi. I am Nash," he said again.

I snap out of it and feeling very embarrassed, scrapping all the words together I could gather. I take a step back.

"Hi... I am Kallie."

My dog starts to growl, "This is Maverick."

I stare back at Maverick. I look back at Nash again, taking in his eyes. He has this smirk on his face. It is hard to read what he is thinking.

"He—he is usually friendly."

Nash smiles back at me; I noticed how white his teeth were.

"It is nice to meet you, Kallie."

Nash, bending over to sticking his hand out to Maverick, "Nice to meet you too, Maverick." Maverick, being friendly as always, allows Nash to pet his head.

I need to escape this embarrassment. I look so stupid right now. I asset the situation again. I have to end this and try to meet him again once I can get myself together. I glance at my watch, trying not to seem too interested in this situation.

"It was nice to meet you. I have to go. I have class soon." My voice is louder than I expected.

Franticly, trying to get myself together, and salvage this situation, I go to shut the door. Nash, who is still bent over an arm halfway through my front door. Nash quickly pulls back his arm.

I stood there in shock at what had just happened. I realized that I could not open the front door to leave due to that embarrassing introduction. I went to the peak hole in the door. I see Nash standing up and collecting himself. I watched through the blinds as he turned away to start walking back to his house.

I stepped outside through my back door. I looked around the corner to see if he was still there. He smiled. I turned to look at maverick, staring at him I tell him, "Nash smiled." I am ecstatic. I ran up the stairs to my bedroom. I quickly did my hair and makeup and looked around my room for a clean shirt that was not stained. I grabbed my keys and gave my dog a pat on the head, telling him goodbye for the day. I stuck my hand out to grab the doorknob, when I remembered the awkward situation that had happened minutes ago. I could not pull myself together to open this door. I decided I would go out the back door and walk around to my car. I knew this would be a better choice than opening the front door for Nash to see me.

I look at my phone and realized I was running late. I ran out the back door, slamming it behind me. Walking as fast as my legs could carry me, I turned the corner of my house and saw my black Mustang. Hopping into my driver's seat and starting my ignition, I looked out the window. I see Nash again. He looks like he lives alone. One tan leather couch, a few boxes and a couple of bags of clothes. I started to back out my driveway when Nash notices me leaving. He gives me a smile and a wave as I drive away. I keep looking for the woman to arrive. I just can't imagine with how they look that they aren't a couple.

I live in a small town in Iowa. It has three major roads. In the town, we have a coffee shop on the third. My house is right next door to the bar on First Street. The other side of my house is Nash's house. On Second Street is the post office. Everyone really does know everyone. I have to drive 20 minutes to get to a town that leads to an interstate.

I arrive on campus. I have British Literature. This class is so boring and at the most inconvenience time. I rush into the building. I look around for Holden. I debate if I even want to tell him about my morning as I walk next to him. He does look like he needs a laugh today.

"Holden, you are never going to believe my morning. I have a new neighbor, and he is so gorgeous."

He laughs. "Did you talk to him?"

I smile awkwardly. "Well, he saw me watching from my window. So, he came over to say hi, but I almost slammed his arm in the door while petting Maverick."

I watch Holden laugh a little too loud. After he collects his self, I tell him even more about the terrible meeting with Nash.

"So, you think you will talk to him again?"

"I don't know. I think I ruined our first meeting."

I walk into my classroom; Holden keeps walking past it. It is so embarrassing to admit how I met my new neighbors. But maybe if he is single, he will find my awkwardness cute?

I try to focus on the lecture today. It was hard to focus when I can't stop playing back the meeting with Nash. I hope when I do get home, Nash isn't home. After class I tell Holden bye. On my way home, I decided to stop by my favorite coffee shop. An afternoon picks me up sounds great right now. Also, a nap sounds great too. I wish I didn't have so much homework to do. My analysis is due tomorrow and I have not even started it. I know I am going to need coffee.

I realized I was close to my exit. They lost me in the music and my thoughts. I take the exit and drive to the coffee shop.

I walk carefully inside since it is snowing hard now. Ordering an extra-large vanilla latte, I wait quietly for my drink to be ready. On my walk to my car, I notice the snow was piling up. I'd say it is about two inches deep now. I drive carefully the five minutes to my home.

Maverick is waiting by the back door. For a lab, he loves to play in the snow. I throw his ball a few times as I sip on my coffee. I leave the back door cracked for him as I go inside to finally writing my papers for school.

Maverick's barking startles me. I open the front door; Nash is standing there.

"Hey," I whispered.

He is wearing a light blue T-shirt that looks good with his eyes. My eyes lock on his. I take in his face. I stare at his brown eyes, the slope of his nose. The way he smirks when he smiles.

"Hey," he says.

I realize it is still snowing. "Come in."

"Do you mind if I borrow a cup of coffee?"

"No, I mean yes. You can have a cup of coffee." I said as I giggle.

I walk to the kitchen, with Nash following me. I watch as he observes my home. "Would you like a quick tour?"

"That would be nice. I like seeing how the older houses were made."

"I love the history of this house. It was built in the 1800s. Upstairs and downstairs makes a circle. The entry way has the stairs; you can also go left or right. Left takes you to the dining room, then the living room, next is the kitchen, and a bathroom follow by the office back to the entryway."

Nash put his hands on his hips. "Oh, this is unique."

I nod, "The stairs to the basement are actually on the kitchen floor. You lift it up."

He looks curious. "What is upstairs?"

I gently smile, "Four bedrooms and a laundry room, which also makes a circle."

"Let's go back to the kitchen," I tell him. I open my black cabinet to grab two coffee mugs. I watch as his eyes look around the room and back at me. I cannot take the silence anymore.

"Is that your mustang?" I ask.

"Yes, she is my drag car."

I turn to look at him and he noticed the pictures of Holden and me on the wall.

"Is that your boyfriend?"

I watch him pull his lip to his teeth.

"No, that is Holden. He's my best friend."

"Oh, that's cool."

He crosses his arms to face me. I back away and quickly change the subject.

"Why are you moving to a new house?" I ask.

"I wanted to move out of the city."

I try to find something to talk about.

"What do you do for work?"

He pauses and smiles. "I am a welder."

"Was the woman your wife?"

"Nope, she is the realtor," he said popping the P in nope.

I watch as he finishes his coffee. His small talk is ridiculous. The more I want to find out about him, the more he doesn't go into detail with my questions.

"Thank you for the coffee, Kallie." He smiles at me.

"You're welcome. You can stop by anytime." I walk him to the front door and lock it behind him.

Second encounter with Nash wasn't as bad. It was still weird. I can't believe I let a stranger to tour my house. I shake my head. I need to get back to my homework.

After I was done with my homework, I decided to go play outside with Maverick. I put on my university pull over. I slip on my converse before opening the door to let Maverick out. I see Nash outside in his garage. He looks over and sees my Labrador.

"Can I pet your dog?"

I look at Maverick. "Yes, he loves the attention."

He gets down on Maverick level. I watch as Maverick takes the attention. You can almost see him smiling at Nash.

Nash suddenly looks up at me. "Are you available on Saturday?"

"Yes," I said so gently.

"Would you like to go out for coffee or dinner?"

"Dinner sounds wonderful. Does 7 work?" I said.

"Yes, see you later, Kallie."

Hearing the way, he says my name makes my heart skip a beat. I am so nervous. Maverick wants back inside. I slowly walk to my door. I look at my phone to realize tomorrow is Saturday. I decided to watch a movie downstairs. I forget movies make me so sleepy.

I walk up to my bedroom. I look out the window to see how much snow is on the ground now. I noticed Nash also does not have curtain put up yet. I step back so if he looks out his windows, he couldn't see me. I admire my view once again before going to bed.

I wake up kind of late today. It is 11:30. I hear Maverick still snoring. I roll over and he is next to my bed. I grab my phone to check notifications. Of course, all texts from Holden.

Holden: Are you awake yet?

Me: just waking up now.

Holden: Hang out tonight?

Me: Can't. Date with Nash.

My phone instantly starts ringing.

"You have a date with Nash already?" Holden said.

"I'm not ugly, just a little awkward."

I listen to him talk about his plans for tonight. It makes me happy tonight is my date night. Throw on a jacket and walk downstairs. I slide my shoes on to take Maverick outside. I should have got dressed. I look over. Nash and his friends are staring at me. I watch them out of the corner of my eye. Nash keeps glancing over at me and his friend. All I can think is I should have put pants on, not just an oversize jacket. I watch Nash walk to me.

"No pants?" Nash smirks.

"I wasn't thinking. I usually just take Maverick out like this in the morning."

I observe his smirk.

"I should be going inside now." I said.

"I can't wait to see you tonight." He said.

I usually wear a cardigan and skinny jeans, but tonight is our date. I pick out v neck black lace long sleeves black dress, and ankle booties. He picks me up in his white F150 truck. I give it to that man; he sticks to one specific car brand. I cannot say much I also drive a Ford, and probably always will.

"We are going to a place I think you will like."

I smile at him, "Great."

It's a white tablecloth restaurant. I have never been to one before. He orders a bottle of white wine. I, in fact, do not like fancy, I am too messy for white tablecloth.

Dinner is going well. I am super nervous. I keep biting my lip. I wish I knew what he was thinking. He keeps just staring at me and smiling. I feel like a million of butterflies are swirling around inside my stomach.

"What would you like to order?"

"I am a simple girl. I want pasta."

I listen as he orders for me. His voice is deep. Our food finally arrives. It looks delicious. The Alfredo sauce is super creamy and thick. I don't want to sit in silence, so I have to make a conversation. I also don't want to show how messy of an eater I am. I try to eat slowly.

"Do you have any family around here, Nash?"

"I have a half-sister, Willow."

"Oh, I have an older sister." I half smile.

I do not want to ask too many questions. No one likes nosy people. He also doesn't answer all my questions.

We finish our meal and I finish the bottle of wine. I didn't notice he only had a glass. I

Nash looks at me, half smiling, "Are you ready to go home?"

I sigh because I am not ready for tonight to be over.

I smile back, "Yeah, I am. Thank you for dinner."

We walk to the truck. He opens the door for me to get in. I can't stop making eye contact with him. Every time we lock eyes, my stomach feels like it has a million of butterflies. Nash starts to talk more.

"Do you always take a long time to talk?" I asked flatly.

"Yes, I like to listen more than I speak."

Nash pulls into my driveway. Quickly, he jumps out of the truck to open my door. We walk together to my front door.

"I could have walked here from your house."

"It is way too cold, and that is so rude to make you walk."

I start to smile, then I was worried I might have food in my teeth. I just want to kiss him so badly. I control myself because I don't know if he kisses on the first date.

"I really should go inside," I sigh.

"Ok, can I see you again like tomorrow?

"Absolutely. I'll be home all day."

I turn away so slowly. I panicked and slammed the door in his face. I can't believe I just slammed the door in his face. I pull out my phone. It is 10:00. I change into my pajamas and decide to watch a rom com movie. I hear my phone ding. It is from Nash. Have a great night. I cannot wait to see you tomorrow. I smile at my phone, like he can see it.

The next morning, I see his lights on. I decided to get dressed. I casually walk over to his house. I ring the doorbell. He opens the door in his pajama pants. My eyes trace his body, casually stopping at his abs before looking back into his eyes. I know he noticed by the grin on his face.

"Would you like to go to coffee and books coffee shop?" I pause, "It is my favorite place, and who does not like mornings when you do not have to make your own coffee?"

"Yes, make yourself at home while I get dressed."

He leaves to his bedroom. I start looking around the living room. I noticed a bookcase with boxes in front of it. He likes books, so that is something we have in common. Then I notice a photo of him and the coffee shop girl. He comes downstairs dressed and ready to go.

"I will drive. The truck is better in the snow than the Mustang."

I just nodded as I turned on my toes.

The drive to the coffee shop is quiet. It is the only coffee place in town. It is a charming small town coffee shop. The bistro tables have candles on them. The side wall is floor to ceiling bookshelves full of books.

I ordered a white chocolate mocha, and he orders black coffee. I smile and offer to pay. He refused to let me pay and paid. We sit down at a small table next to the window.

"Why do you have a photo of the coffee shop owner on your bookcase?"

Nash laughs, "That is my sister, Willow. It was taken when she opened this place."

"No way! This is my favorite coffee shop."

Willow is so different from Nash. She has long blond hair, and blue eyes. She is not as tan or as tall as Nash.

"The bookshelves are full of books from the classics to more recent, most of these books are from Willow's personal collection."

"That's pretty cool, I didn't know that."

"Yeah, Willow had a dream for anyone to be able to enjoy coffee and books."

I hate small talk, but I feel a deep urge to know Nash better. I need to get him alone and find out more. I am awkward getting to know new people. I never knew the baristas name was Willow. I come here every morning, usually in a rush.

"Kallie, want to go back to my house?"

"Oh absolutely."

I walk to the truck, and he opens the door for me. I have never actually had anyone open my car door before. He helps me in. I watch him walk to his side of the truck. He starts the truck and begins to drive home. He keeps looking at me. I have no idea what to say.

"What type of music do you listen to?" I asked.

"Country, what about you?"

"A little bit of everything but punk is my favorite."

He turns on a country play list on Spotify, and it is not terrible. The town is small, so the car ride is not long. I am not really a fan of country music. I look out the window observing the snow drifts.

We arrive at his house. He looks unsure if he wants me to come inside.

"I don't have much inside. Just the basics."

I nod, "That is to be expected you just moved in."

He helps me out of the truck. He opens the door; I notice how bright it is in here. It is a beautiful A frame house. The front has floor to ceiling windows. The stairs are in front of the entry way.

"Would you like to sit down?" I nod and sit down on his tan couch.

"I am going to start a fire, if you want to watch TV While I get it going."

"Yeah, it's pretty cold outside."

The TV Is right above his fireplace. It is a beautiful view. I start to laugh as Nash struggles to get the fire started. He assures me he can start a fire. I start to lose hope on the fire, until a little spark finally came. I move closer to the fireplace to warm my hands. I am still so cold.

"Let me show you the house, it's an impressive little house."

"It's so beautiful with the bright light coming in and how dark it is also."

"This is the worst part of the house, wait until you see upstairs."

We walk back to the living room. If this is the worst part, then the upstairs must be amazing.

"This is the guest bathroom; the shower actually looks to your house." Nash smiles.

"Oh, that's good to know." I said.

He starts up the stairs. I noticed the slanted roof has skylights. You can almost see the entire sky.

"Wow, I bet it's beautiful up here at night." I said.

"Yeah, wait until you see my room."

The bathroom has a standalone shower and a beautiful claw-foot bathtub. The whole side of the slanted wall is windows facing the woods.

"The upstairs is way better than the downstairs, trust me." He said.

Through the bathroom is his room. Two slanted windows facing my house.

"Wow, not a lot of privacy with all the windows and the front made of all windows."

"No, not yet. I do plan on hanging curtains at the front of the house to help with privacy."

"It is so different from my old 1880's house. The largest window I have is my bay windows. My regular windows are larger than the average size home they are not floor to ceiling."

Nash smiles at me, "It is a small town, not much traffic, I am not too worried about someone breaking in."

"So does it bother you that this is called the murder house?"

"No. I actually got a good deal on it because they just wanted to sell it."

"Ok. Let me walk you home."

Once we arrive at my front door, he notices I am shaking from being so cold. He pulls me into his arms. He smells so good. I didn't notice before he pulled me in. His body is warm, and I can feel his muscles under his shirt.

"I can't wait to see you again, Kallie."

"Me either, Nash."

I really should go inside. It is getting too cold out here. The snow is falling in my hair. Nash pushes my hair out of my face.

"You have beautiful blue eyes Kallie. What color is that?"

"Thank you, and pale light blue."

"Go inside before you freeze to death."

I open my door and fall against it.

4

Nash

Kallie is beautiful. She is also awkward. The way she looks at me so innocently. I know I can't get close to her. I would only destroy her. When she was in my house, I wanted to grab her by her throat and just kiss her. I was afraid that would scare her off, so I decided to play it cool. Make her want me just as bad as I want her.

This town is small. I am sure it will not be long before she knows about my past. I want to keep from her. I am not as bad as people make me seem. My past is just different from the average. If people only knew the truth about what really happened.

Kallie didn't realize I could see her watching me from the window. I hope she also didn't notice I was still petting her dog when she slammed the door on me. Even with her hair a mess and a stained shirt, she is still beautiful.

It embarrassed me she saw me slip on ice. Everything went everywhere. I think it's funny she slammed the door in my face. I saw her looking around while running to her car. I wonder if she is trying to avoid me. I hope not because I really want to know more about her.

If only I can find a way to make her talk without asking too many questions about me. Is that even possible? I call Willow.

"My new neighbor is Kallie. She was watching me from her window. I slipped on ice. I went to meet her, and she almost slammed the door on my arm."

Willow is laughing too hard to speak.

"It all went down like that?"

"Basically, come over after work."

I decided to unpack my kitchen, while waiting for Willow to get here. It's only a five-minute drive from the coffee shop to my house. Kallie has these English teacups she uses. She doesn't have a normal sized coffee cup. It makes me wonder how many times she has to refill them.

She is a little odd, but I think Kallie could be a fun fling.

"Willow, I don't know what do to. How do I get to know her without her knowing all the bad about me?"

Willow faces me with a serious look on her face, "This town is small, she will find out. However, get her to talk about herself. Avoid any questions that you don't want to answer."

"Wow, that is your great advice. It sucks honestly.

"Do you want help unpacking your kitchen?"

"No, I hope Kallie is home soon."

One thing I do know to be true. She loves to read, maybe I could find out her favorite book. I could buy it. She is an English major. It is probably Austen, Bronte, or someone from the classics. I hope not, they are romantic and that isn't me. I could buy her favorite book and note my favorite quotes from them. That is romantic.

If nothing else maybe I can buy her love.

I hear Jake running through my front door. "I have to see this neighbor. She sounds funny as hell." Now he is being the weird one watching her from my window.

"She has a dog; she is probably playing with him." I try to get him out of the damn window, but he doesn't budge.

"Let's play video games, Jake."

He slowly comes to sit on my couch. "Good news travels fast in this town." I nod. No shit it does.

The town is so small, everyone knows everyone. Which isn't that great when you try to keep your life private. I still have no idea why I came back to this town. It apart of my past but I still feel drawn to this small town.

Our back yards meet at Kallie's fence line. I should get a patio set. I could sit outside every morning waiting for her to let Maverick outside. I just want every chance I have to talk to her.

Jake is still sitting on my couch not reading the room. "How did you hear about my neighbor anyways?"

"I was getting coffee and Willow told me. Of course, I came straight here."

Of course, they talked about my embarrassment. I hear Kallie calling for Maverick, I see Jake jump straight to the window.

"You she can probably see you."

He gives me shrug, "at least I won't have to worry about slipping on ice from here."

I roll my eyes at him.

"That's a good one," I hear Willow yell out.

"You're not that funny."

"I'm not not funny."

I hear them both laughing from the window. I pray at this moment Kallie doesn't notice them staring out the window like stalkers.

"You know she comes to coffee and Books like every day."

I raise my eyebrow up at the comment. I knew she said she loves this place, but I didn't know she frequent there. Good thing I love coffee.

I hold back the information about our date. I know they would lose their minds over that. Especially since I just got back into town.

I try to get them to leave so I can make plans on how I can see her again this morning. I'm Nash Conrad, do I need a reason to do half the things I do? No. The answer is always no. Kallie has the effect over me to where I want to show her how great I can be. The side most people will never see from me. I push Jake and Willow out the front door quickly before they do anything to make me embarrassed. I glare at Jake while he grabs waffles off the table before leaving. I have to have a better impression on this girl. It is now a need not a want.

5

Kallie

The loud knocking at my front door startles me. I thought I was the only one that woke up ridiculously early for no reason. I grab my coffee mug as I walk to my front door.

"I noticed your light was still on."

"Come in."

"Would you like breakfast? I made way too many waffles."

"Yeah, let me grab my shoes."

I walk with Nash to his house. The fresh snow is still fluffy, my shoes are getting filled with snow. I follow behind him as he walks into his house. I slip off my wet, snow-covered shoes by the front door before going to the kitchen.

Nash was not joking; he made a ton of waffles. I observe the two coffee mugs on the table. The large print says Coffee & Books. I wonder how he got them. Nash smiles as he looks at the table full of waffles.

"I like to cook. Sometimes, I forget it is just me." He says hesitantly.

I laugh. His smile makes me smile. I pour coffee into my mug.

"Kallie, you look amazing."

"I doubt it. I feel like I need a shower, and some make up." My voice full of sleep.

"You are naturally beautiful. I did not notice your freckles when you wear makeup."

The silence seems to always follow Nash.

"Kallie, I want to be able to see you anytime I can."

"Is that a statement or a question." I say confidently.

He smiles at me, "Is both an option, I mean only if you want to see me too."

I nod while giggling, "Of course I would like to see you often. I am busy since I am still in college and have an internship and volunteer."

"It's worth being patient for." Nash says as he hands me a plate.

I like when Nash compliments my small features like my freckles. They aren't dark enough to really notice without looking closely. He is being so flirty and cute this morning. I watch as he cleans up his kitchen. I offer to help him. I go to place dishes in the sink for him to wash. He grabs the sprayer. Nash sprays me with water. I try to grab the sprayer from him. I end up in front of the sink with him behind me. I grab his hand. He sprays both of us.

My stomach hurt from laughing so hard.

"I will go get us towels." I watch as Nash leaves the kitchen.

I am really enjoying flirting with Nash. I know it is still early getting to know him, I can't help to but wonder if this will lead to something more. I feel like I have known him for my whole life.

It is time to leave for work. I cannot wait to tell Holden about me weekend. I find Holden's car; I always park next to him. He gets out of his car when he sees me arrive.

"How was your weekend, Kallie?" Holden asks shyly.

I smile huge at Holden, "My weekend was spent with Nash. He literally came over to ask if I wanted waffles this morning because he made so many."

"So can he cook?" Holden asked.

"Yeah, it not too hard to make waffles." I stated.

"I guess you are right. When do you plan to see him again?" Holden crosses his arms.

"I am not sure; I have a busy week. I am sure Nash is going to add to the busy."

"Yeah, he is." Holden says as he looks at me.

I follow Holden in the building. I can't see past his tall statue. I stare at the back of his head; I start to giggle.

"Did you brush your hair this morning." I asked.

"Yeah, but I was wearing a hat."

His dark hair is messy. I like to poke fun at Holden since he is always doing it to me.

"I cannot wait for Friday already," Holden sighs.

"I feel you. I checked my email this morning. I am supposed to edit an 800-page manuscript about birds today. Birds Holden, do you know how boring this sounds." I answered annoyed.

Holden smirks. "I never check my work email before I get here. I rather be surprised on Monday."

I was able to go all day without checking my phone while at work. That is impressive since I read about birds today. I love my job but some of the manuscripts I read are ridiculous. Before I leave, I make plans to study with Holden for the test coming up. I do have to make flash cards when I get home. Holden loves when I make flashcards.

As I drive home, I make a mental note of the materials I need to make flashcards for. I pull into my driveway and notice Nash isn't home yet. I walk inside and quickly greeted by Maverick. We go outside; I throw his ball a few times. His paws must be cold because he already wants to come inside. I sit on my couch while making study guides and flash cards.

My alarms wake me up. I didn't realize I fell asleep while making flash cards. I wake up in a panic. I start to make a note of everything I need to do this week. Since Nash moved in next door, I have been a little distracted from school. I go to class but procrastinate on doing homework or studying. Work is time consuming. I love working, but hate I only get to spend 3 days a week there. I often have to bring work home with me to meet deadlines. I rush to get dressed and make coffee. I have three minutes to spare before I have to leave.

No surprise I am looking for my keys. I am always losing them. I text Holden to let him know I will be about 5 minutes late. I finally find my keys. I pet Maverick's head, "be back later." I try to start my car and it does not start. I should really invest in a new car, but I really love this car despite how much it breaks. It is only 5 years old. I open my hood to find the issues. I hear a man behind me speaking.

"Do you need help?" I gasp.

I turn around to respond and see who is standing behind me. It is the same guy I saw at Nash's house. I lower my defenses.

"Maybe, I was trying to leave but my car is not turning on." I said.

"Let me check it out by the way, I am Jake. Nash's friend."

Jake is equally as handsome. His blue eyes are icy and clear. They are so beautiful. He towers over my small stature. He is at least six foot three.

"Thanks Jake." I smile at him.

I go back inside to make Jake coffee. It is bitterly cold outside in January. I walk back out with coffee.

"I found what is wrong with your car, it is your alternator." He explained.

I watch Jake leave to get my new part for my car. Nash is outside. I grab my phone from my car. I text Holden.

Me: Jk car broke again. Nash's friend is fixing it.

Holden: kk. Let me know if you need help.

Jake returns and Nash still does not come over. I go outside. I stare Nash down. He avoids looking at me. He just observed Jake. I glance down at Jake.

"I'll have this in in a few minutes and your car will work just fine." Jake says.

"Ok if you need anything I will be inside studying." I smile at Jake.

I look out the window. Jake and Nash are both working on my car. Nash knocks on my door. "Hey, your car is fixed."

"Thank you, how much do I owe Jake?" I asked.

Nash grins, "Don't worry about it, Kallie."

I nod "Thank you. But you didn't have to do that."

"I wanted too."

I give Nash a quick hug and he helps me in my car. I watch him as I back out and leave.

Once I arrive, I park next to Holden's car. I scan the library for Holden. I pull out my books and laptop. I place my phone on do not disturb; while doing so, I see a message from Nash.

Nash: Is your car, ok?

Me: Yes, I am studying. I will text you later.

"This morning was eventful Holden. My car wouldn't start. Jake and Nash fixed my car." I explained to Holden.

Holden glances at me "You should think about getting a new car."

"I love this car."

I watch as Holden laughs. "Kallie, it is always breaking."

"I know, I will think about getting a new one.

We start studying. I lay the flash cards on the table.

"I made you a set color coded by time periods."

I pull out my phone, it feels like we have been here for hours.

"It's getting late I should go home." I tell Holden.

"Do not forget we have volunteer hours tomorrow," Holden reminds me.

I smile and nod. I completely forgot about story time tomorrow. I gather my stuff as I stand up. Holden reaches to give me a hug bye, as we walk to our cars.

I take a deep breath as I pull into my driveway. I really wish I had a garage. I see someone standing in my doorway. Nash comes to opens my car door.

"Hey Nash, what are you doing here?" I across my arms.

"I wanted to see you and check on your car. Jake is a decent mechanic, I just wanted to see if anything else needs repairs."

"It's almost dark, it can wait until morning." I huffed.

He grabs my wrist, "Kallie, go on a real date with me. Not like coffee or dinner but a real date."

"Right now?"

"Yes, just grab a thick jacket not a cardigan."

I rush upstairs to grab a jacket.

"Where are we going?" I asked.

"It's a surprise you will like it." Nash responded.

He starts to walk to his truck, and I follow behind. I climb into his truck. He turns the music on softly playing in the background.

"What's your favorite book Kallie?"

I laugh. "That is a hard question." I take a moment to gather my thoughts.

"I like a few classics and I read a lot of current books. But if I had to stay a favorite then I would pick Looking for Alaska."

"Do you have a favorite book?" I asked Nash.

"Yes, actually." He nods.

We reach our destination. It's dark and cold.

I turn to look at him, "you brought me to an old farm in winter."

"Yes, I did." I watch as he lays out a blanket in the bed of his truck and motions for me to climb in.

"I brought all your favorites; coffee, coffee cakes and fruit." Nash points to the basket.

Nash is looking at me so passionately, "This is my favorite place, you can see the stars for miles. No light polluting the second most beautiful thing ever." He says.

I sip my coffee "What is the first most beautiful thing?"

"You." He said so confidently.

I gasp at his words.

He leans in slowly, his hands placed on both sides of my face. Nash slowly kisses me. I feel our tongues swirling around each other. He is breathing heavy. His fingers are combing my auburn hair. There is no one around for miles. He pulls away. He hands me my coffee. I grab it with both hands. He passes me a cinnamon coffee cake. I barely noticed how cold I am with his arms wrapped around me. I take a mental photo of this moment. I look into his eyes. How can one man be so handsome? I ask myself. Nash moves closer to me. He envelopes me into his arms. I can feel his breath on my neck. I am taken back when he places a simple kiss on the side of my neck.

"Nash, I am freezing. Can we go back now?" I finished my coffee and all I have is my jacket and Nash keeping me warm.

"Start the truck and I will clean up." He hands me the keys.

I get into the truck and start it. Nash throws everything into the back seat. On the drive home, he reaches for my hand. Nash glances over at me.

This is a dangerous situation I am in. I can't sleep. I keep replaying tonight in my head. Tonight was magical. I was everything I ever dreamed about. Nash is so romantic. When I am with him, I feel like only I matter.

"Stay with me tonight, Kallie."

"What? It hasn't been that long." I said.

"Alright." Nash nods his head slowly.

We are almost at my house. I look over at him, "I changed my mind. I will stay with you tonight." I exclaimed.

Nash takes me by the hand to his bedroom. I watch him take off his shirt. I admire his tattoos. He starts to take off his pants. I close my eyes as he changes into his pajama pants. I move closer to him.

"What are your tattoos?" I asked.

He shows me his back. I trace over the stormy sky with a ship on it. He turns back to face me. Anatomical heart over his heart. Birds at his hip bone and his last name down his ribs.

"Why is the ship on your back and the map on your forearm?" Curiosity shows on my face.

"It made sense at the time." Nash shrugs.

"Fair enough." I nod back.

I climb into his bed. He lays next to me. I place my head on his chest. He combs his fingers through my hair. He gently kisses the top of my head.

My alarm is blaring to wake me up. I look over to see Nash is still sleeping so I decided to leave. I go home and get dressed, I am ready for work with my usual v neck, cardigan, and skinny jeans. I grab my favorite coffee mug. I pour my coffee slip on my converse and off to the office I go.

Holden appears to be in good mood this morning, "Kallie, I brought coffee!"

I laugh, "You must have read my mind Holden! It was a long night."

Holden glances over to my desk. "Oh, Nash again?"

I can feel my cheeks turning red. "Yes. He took me to an old farm at night. It was actually romantic."

Holden is laughing, "I could never take anyone to an old farm, that is so corny."

"Yeah, kind of but like I found it actually nice."

Holden is laughing harder at this point, "You really should date more. I promise, there are way better dates than a farm."

I start to laugh, "Yeah, you right."

We get back to doing work. I see Holden glancing over at me still laughing. One wonderful thing about being interns, Holden and I share an office. Two desks crammed into one smallish office. After graduation I will miss this. The past two years I have been in this office with my best friend.

"Have you applied for graduation yet?" Holden has a smirk on his face.

I glance back at Holden. "Well, I printed the application, I need to fill it out an submit it. So no, I have not yet. I should graduate in May."

"It is only February; you do have time. I just know you forget about everything." I watch Holden lean back into his chair.

I look at Holden, "I guess I am scared to graduate. We have to find a job if our internship doesn't offer us a position. The what ifs are scary."

"It's not always supposed to be easy, Kallie. The challenges in life, that what makes people grow and adapt." Holden crosses his arms.

"I know but it is still scary. How does anyone expect a 22-year-old to have their future planned. I don't even know what I want for dinner most nights." I say.

"I know what you mean."

I am not ready to graduate. The thought of find a real job is terrifying. I like my internship; I hope it will turn into a full-time job. I know I will not always work with Holden so it is nice to have a friend I can work with.

Sadly, I know the real word isn't quite like being interns.

"Do you think we will get an offer after graduation?" Holden asks.

I lean back in my chair," I hope so Holden. I don't really have a different plan."

"My goal is to keep working here. I really like it." I tell him.

I look up from my computer. "That would be a dream."

It is finally my break time. I noticed Nash standing at the front office waiting for me. "Nash, what are you doing here?"

He giggles. "I thought we could go to lunch together."

I walk with him to his car. He helps me into his car. I noticed he already got my coffee order. It is a little too silent. "Nash, I don't have a long break. Is everything ok?"

"Yes, I just needed to see you." I smile.

I really don't fully understand Nash. He can be so playful and yet so mysterious at the same time. He only ever wants to talk about me and my life. Yet, I don't know a whole lot about him. Nash walks me back to my office. He glares at Holden. Holden's eyes lock on Nash. I feel Nash's hand on my lower back, he gives me a small kiss, and tells me bye.

"That was weird." Holden said.

My voice is flat. "I mean he get jealous of other guys around me."

"No, I think that is possession." Holden responds.

I try to shake off the judgmental look Holden is giving me. It is going to be a long day at the office. I dive into reading and editing. Maybe Holden a valid point. Nash might be possessive of me. I can't help but to think Holden is wrong. I need him to be wrong, it's a few weeks and I still know nothing.

After work I invite Nash over. I make us the only meal I can, pasta. He walks through the front door. I watch Maverick run to him as I make my way to the front door.

"I made us dinner." He smiles.

"Thank you, I am starving." I smile back at him.

After we finish eating helps me clean up the kitchen. It is already late. I glance at the clock. It is midnight.

Nash grabs my hand, "Dance with me Kallie."

I turn on a slow song. We dance around the kitchen; he spins me around. I lay my head on his chest. Our bodies feel like one dancing together.

"Will you stay with me tonight?" I ask.

"I would love too." He kisses my forehead.

I am falling for this man quickly. I feel like I am floating on the clouds. I take Nash to my bedroom. I watch him take off his shirt. I stare his body down. He climbs into my bed, motioning me to join him. I roll to face him.

"Are you ready for tomorrow?" I asked.

He looks at me confused. "What is tomorrow."

"It's your birthday silly." I laugh.

"Oh. I didn't know you knew this." His face seems surprised.

"I may not know much about you, but I do know your birthday." I tell Nash.

I text Nash's sister Willow. "Thank you for telling me about Nash's birthday." That is probably one good thing about going to Coffee and Books so much. I wonder how much she knows about me and Nash. I would assume a lot since he does seem close to his sister.

6

Nash

I am more than annoyed. Willow told Kallie my birthday is tomorrow. I didn't want to go out for it. It's not a special birthday. I will be 23. I guess any chance I get to see Kallie is a special day. It has to mean something that she stayed at my place and now I am in her bed. How much longer can I keep my past life a secret from her? In this town, probably not long at all.

We finally had our first kiss. It still shocks me that she placed a kiss on my neck. I wanted to grab her and fuck her right there. I know she would freak out being out in the open. It was freezing out there. I would have kept her warm.

I keep seeing her phone light up. I don't want to wake her to see who could be texting her at this house. I glance at my phone. It is just pasted midnight. I have a feeling it is Holden. I don't even know why she likes the guy. His beady stare gives me a feeling he's up to no good and I refuse to let him take Kallie. I try to keep remember they are friends, but they are always together.

I know I should try to go to sleep and enjoy having Kallie in my arms. It's kind of hard when her stupid phone won't stop. I am surprised her phone doesn't wake her up. I grit my teeth; I feel Kallie starting to shift her legs around me. My mind wonders if she would want to be woken up by me. Probably not. I lay here memorized by her touch.

I am two seconds from grabbing her phone when I feel her move so slightly.

"Are you still awake?" Kallie whispers.

"Yes."

I feel her press her body deeper into mine. I hold on to her tighter, making her feel safe and secure but also wanting her to go back to sleep. I get the feeling Kallie thought going to the farm was stupid. It was bad on my part with how cold it was. I just wanted her to show her what makes me think of her. This woman makes me want to move mountains for her.

Kallie has no idea how amazing she is. She is beautiful, smart, caring. Kind of funny but cornier. I have this overwhelming feeling to protect her from myself while also pulling her towards me. It just feels like everything I touch makes everything burn. I don't want her burnt. I will burn for her, and I refuse to burn for anyone.

I wake to Kallie is already gone. I am grateful she let me sleep in, but I would have liked to be woken up by her. I slide my pants back on and rub my hands through my hair. I need coffee and a shower. I head straight to Coffee and Books.

"Large Coffee."

"Are you paying this time?"

"Willow, don't start."

She rolls her eyes and I chuckle at her. I wait for my coffee to be made, noticing how busy it is in here.

"Here Nash."

"Ya know I might actually pay if I got better service."

"Never."

I maybe the older sibling but she defiantly acts older than me. I watch Willow doing what she loves, and it makes me happy. I give her smile before I head out.

I get into my truck and start driving I have flash back of seeing Jake talking to her about her car being broken set a rage in me. I know he wouldn't do any harm on her but apart me is jealous that he was able to help her. I saw the way he looked and her and worst the way she looked back at him. She quickly fixed her face. I paid for Jake picking up the parts for her car, a part of me wished I was the one to fix it. I look over at Jake he is still grinning.

"This is pissing us both off and this damn part will not come lose."

I see Jake steps ahead of making his way up the steps to the kitchen. He grabs two beers out of the fridge. I really should put them in the garage. I slide on the counter.

"You and Kallie have any plans tonight?"

"I don't think so."

I see him eyeing me. I can feel the question he is burning to ask. I shoot him a look and just like that he changes the subject.

We sit in silence for what feels like an eternity.

"Did you want to go out?"

"Yeah, kind of."

"Alright I'll ask her."

I slide off the counter. I need to finish this car. I hear Jake's out steps behind me. His clown feet are loud marching down the steps. I pick up my wrench and get back to work. I hear Jake cussing more and louder. A chuckle escapes without thinking about it.

"Where you mad when you put this back together?"

"Hell, yeah I was."

We finally get the car apart and start working on replacing parts. Write on the board in the garage to get more NOS.

My mind starts wondering about having her next to me while racing. I wonder if she will even like it or even knows what drag racing is. She is not the type to go to races for no reason. I can see her now bring a book because she finds it boring. A smile starts to form at the thought. Having her in my car, staring at me while I am driving. Her blue eyes sucking the soul out of my body. Fuck, I need to see her.

"Are we done?"

I glance up to see Jake staring down on me., "Yeah, for now."

I watch him leave out of the garage.

I got upstairs to lie on the couch. I love days when I don't have work, but I hate how busy Kallie is. I am sure she is in class or at work, wasting time away before she is back with me. Happy birthday to me.

7

Kallie

Today is Nash's birthday. I am making him a cake while he is at work. I hear my phone buzzing.

Nash: Tomorrow me and my friends are going to the bar for my birthday. Want to join me?

Me: Yes, what time?

Him: I will pick you up at 7.

I remembered when Nash was working on his Mustang. I noticed his tools were on the ground. With that knowledge, I decided a toolbox would be the best gift. I have to go to class soon. I really don't want to go.

I decided to skip class and go to shopping for the toolbox for Nash.

I love the way snow looks while it is falling. It is a view you can see every year and never gets old. I just really hate driving in the snow. I finally arrive and pick up a black toolbox to match the mustang. I struggle to stick it in the backseat of my mustang. I have no idea how to wrap it or get it inside my house. Nash should still be sleeping since he worked last night. I get it inside my house and am so excited I cannot wait to show him. My phone starts ringing.

"Hey, I'm awake. Can I come over and have coffee with you?"

"Of course you can." I respond.

I am giving him his gift early. There is no way I can hide this until tonight.

Barely awake, Nash is knocking on the door. I rush to the door; I smile as I open it.

"Hey Love." He greets me with a kiss like always.

"Hey handsome. Ok that was corny, come in Nash." I laugh.

I close the door behind him.

"I got you a birthday present." I said.

"You didn't have too," he responds.

I go to show him where it is.

"This is the best gift I ever got! Thank you so much Kallie." He smiles, "I needed a toolbox. I never got around to buying one."

"You're welcome." He gives me a hug.

"I can't believe you did this for me. No one ever gives me anything".

I walk him to the kitchen. "There is more."

"I also made you a cake."

I covered the cake with a lot of icing since I burnt the cake part. I cut us a slice to give to Nash. I watch Nash look at it.

"You really do not have to eat it. It will not hurt my feelings." I tell him.

"No, I want to. I am sure it will be good."

I watch him take a huge bite. He is trying so hard not to make faces.

"I really tried." I giggled.

"It is the thought that counts, Kallie." I clear the table as I watch Nash walk to the living room.

He sits down on the couch; I bring us coffee. I place the cups on my coffee table; I lean into Nash. I feel him kiss the top of my head; he looks down at me,

"Kallie, I love you." That took me by surprise.

I gasp, "Nash, I love you too."

"No, seriously Kallie, I've never felt this way about anyone before. I go to bed thinking of you. I wake up thinking about you. Everything I do is to be a better person for you."

I start walking to the shower. "I need to go take a shower before we go out.

I try to find something to wear. My favorite ripped skinny jeans and a black V-neck sweater. I lock my eyes on him. He pulls his shirt over his head. I let out a huff.

"You ready to leave?" He glanced over at me.

"As ready as I can be." I said.

I rush to the truck. It is so cold outside. I admire the view as he drives us downtown. He follows the path next to the river. The lights shining on the water make Iowa seem so magical. We finally arrive at the bar. Nash helps me out. I take his hand as we walk towards the bar.

I walk into the bar; The music is so loud. I start to look for Jake. I follow behind Nash. It is so busy tonight.

"I see Jake over by the pool table." I point to Jake.

Do you want to go see them first?" Nash asked me.

"Yeah, who is them?" I asked confused.

"Bree is Jakes girlfriend. Then we can get a drink." Nash confirms.

I sit down across from Bree. Nash sits beside me. The tension at the table is thick. I feel like I am missing something.

"I am going to go order us a drink. What do you want, Kallie?" Nash asked me.

"I want a bud light please." I smile back at him.

Jake tries to make small talk with me. I get the feelings he knows more about Nash and me than he leads on. I can feel Bree silently judging me. I cross my arms as I lean back in my chair. Nash quickly came to my side by drinks in hand.

Nash gives me my drink. He is standing next to Jake. I lock my eyes with Nash. He is smirking. I start talking to Bree, then I hear Nash. "Kallie, will you dance with me?"

"Yes, Nash."

He takes me to the dance area. "You look so good tonight."

I smile, "Thank you." The song is over, Nash leads me back to Jake and Bree.

Nash grabbing our drinks, "It is crowded. Let's move outside." I walk next to Jake as I try to catch up with Nash. My legs are so cold, it's bitterly cold outside. I look over to see Bree looking me up and down. I feel so uncomfortable. I lean into Nash's neck, "Can we go now?"

He grins. "I will go pay the tab."

I walk with him to the bar. He pays the tab and grabs my hand. He leads me outside. He doesn't say a word. All I can hear is my teeth hitting together.

I get into his truck. "Are you ok?" He asks.

"Yeah, I was so cold, and I felt like Bree has an issue with us."

He looks over at me. "She does, but don't worry about it. I would never let anything happen to you."

We are almost home. I just want to be in his arms all night.

"Can I stay over?" I asked quietly.

"I would like that."

The way he looks at me makes me weak. His honey eyes make it hard to say no. The way he looks at me makes me weak.

"What do you want to do?" He glances at me.

"I don't care. Do you want to watch a movie?" I suggest.

"Yeah, pick one."

I suddenly woke up. I was snuggled with Nash. I look to see if he is still asleep. I kiss him gently on the forehead. I watch him move a little.

"Do you want to move to my bed?" I asked, half asleep.

"Yeah." Nash mumbles.

Half asleep we both stumble to my bed. I take off my jeans and switch into my pajamas. I watch him get undressed. I pull the blankets back. Nash reaches for me. He has one arm under me, and one wrapped around my back. I hear his heart beating. It is so calming; I close my eyes. I hear Nash mumble "I love you.' I nod my head back.

My alarm goes off way to early. I have volunteer hours today. Holden and I are doing our children's reading today. It is close to Valentine's Day, so we are reading a story about valentine's day and doing a craft with hearts. Holden is helping me set up when I notice Nash standing behind me. Nash looks incredibly angry when he realized I still volunteer with Holden.

"Nash, this is Holden." I introduce them.

Nash looks at me, "you still work him." More of a statement that a question.

"Yes, he is my best friend."

Nash leans in to give me a kiss "Brought coffee from Coffee and Books."

I watch as Nash turns and walks away. Holden share a look with me half judgment and half understanding.

"Does Nash always act this way?" Holden asked.

"No, Holden not always.

"He saw our photo in my kitchen. Now he is jealous."

"That does make sense." Holden sighs.

Holden would be dressed nice today. He is usually a nice dresser. His perfectly brown hair and blue eye. He wore a white button-down shirt. His sleeves are rolled to his elbows. It does look good on Holden.

I put on my best smile as I read to the children today. I watch Holden take a small group to do a craft. Holden is craftier than me. After the event, Holden helps me clean the library. My coffee is cold now, but I finally have time to drink it. Holden walks me to my car; I am so ready to go home.

I arrive back at my house. The whole way home, not really knowing how to explain Holden to Nash. I see his truck is home. I text Nash. We need to talk about Holden. He is just a friend. I leave my phone on the kitchen counter. Looking out the window, I get lost in my thoughts until my phone buzzes. I am sorry about how I reacted. I hate seeing you with any other man. Forgive me Kallie. This is ridiculous. I take a sharp inhale before I respond back. I forgive you Nash. Come over?

Within minutes, he is at my door. Takes me by the waist, pressing me against the wall.

"I am so sorry Kallie for not trusting you." He leans in for a kiss.

"Nash, seriously, it is okay, but you have to stop being so jealous of Holden." The frustration is thick in my voice.

"Kallie, I am falling even more in love with you; I am just scared to lose you."

I softly smile at Nash, "I am not going anywhere."

"Want to get coffee?" Nash asks.

"Yeah sure."

After a long silence I tell Nash, "It is Valentine's Day."

A smug look on his face. I know I made reservations for eight at our favorite place." My heart melted. We go inside the coffee shop. A black-haired woman with a toddler is staring at Nash. He glances over but make no effort to speak to her. I shake off the weird feeling I have. It makes me uncomfortable her just looking at us. I wonder if Nash knows her. I step up to order. Willow takes our order, "An extra-large white chocolate mocha and large black coffee."

"Anything for my favorite customers". Willow responds.

I observe how Willow interacts with the woman. I hear Willow call her Emma. Willow seems to know her from the way she is speaking to her. I watch her stand across the room from Nash. Willow calls our names for our drink order. Nash gives Emma one last glance before we walk out.

We go home and I get dressed in black lacy dress.

"You look amazing." He looks my body up and down and with a smirk.

"I have a gift for you." I watch as he picks up a perfectly wrapped box. I carefully open the box. I am taken by surprise.

"You got me new heels?" I covered my mouth.

"Yes, I did." Nash is smiling from ear to ear.

"Nash, these are so expensive." I try to hand them back to Nash.

"It is fine. I saw these and they reminded me of you."

I try to hide my excitement.

I love the shoes. They are black with silver studs. I take off my old heels to but on the new ones. I don't wear heels often, so it was also a nice surprise to get new ones.

"Do you want to come back to my house?" He is staring at me waiting for an answer.

"Yes, I would love that." I smirk.

To my surprise, Nash made us a candlelit dinner. He made pasta and of course has red wine already set. I like the small things Nash does.

"I thought we could have a romantic night in." Nash explains.

"I thought you made reservation at our favorite place."

"I did, but I wanted something more romantic." Nash smirks.

After dinner, I walk towards him. He pulls me into to him kissing my forehead. He grabs a book from his bedside table. I cuddle up to him and listens as he reads to me. He has one hand wrapped around me and one holding the book. I am focusing on the sound of his heartbeat; it makes me fall asleep.

I wake up before Nash. I grab my phone to scroll social media. Suddenly, Nash wraps his arms around me.

Nash pulls me in closer, "Would you like to go to the drag strip with me?"

I look at him sideway, "Yes it could be fun."

I bring Nash's coffee to him in the garage.

"I have to register the car when we get there but Jake will be with you."

While he is driving, he takes me hand. I turn the radio down, "How does it work?"

"Two cars are side by side. When the light turns green you go." He smiles at me, "It is a lot of fun and adrenaline rush."

I am nervous. I've been to anything like this before. I sit with Jake. We watch Nash make his first run.

"He started too late." Jake said.

"Oh, I didn't notice." I said.

"Is this your first time here?" Jake chuckled.

"Yeah, it is."

"Are you racing too?"

"Yeah, I am." Jake moves closer to me. I look at him smiling back at me.

"So where is Bree? Does she like racing too?"

"Not really, she doesn't mind coming but also it isn't her favorite."

"That is too bad. I would like to hang out with her."

Jake looks over at me, "I will see if she will come next weekend."

Nash is finally done. I watch him make his way to Jake. He sits between Jake and me. He gives me a quick kiss before turning to Jake.

"What time to you race?" Nash asked.

Jake pulls the paper out of his pocket. "It says at 2. So, I will probably go down soon."

"Do we go against each other?"

I watch them look at their times.

Jake finds it first, "The last one is us."

Nash nod his head. He leans into me. "Are you having fun?"

"I am. It is interesting to watch." I smile.

"Do you want to come with me and Jake?" Nash asked.

"Oh no, I am not ready for that yet." I laughed.

Nash laughs. "I just wanted to ask in case you did want to."

I am not the adrenaline type of girl. I am boring, now that I think about it. I like playing with my dog and reading. That is as boring as it gets. Nash places he hands on my knee. "After this do you want to go back to my house?"

I nod. He can't hear me. It is loud now.

"Jake and I have to go get ready. Will you be ok by yourself or do you want to go down."

I smile, "I will be ok by myself."

It is finally time for Jake and Nash's race. I finally understand what to watch for. I wait for the light to turn green. They both go. Nash appeared to be a half a second later than Jake.

I see them coming back to me. They both are laughing. Jake playfully pushes Nash. I like watching Nash and Jake interact with each other. Their relationship seems like they are closer than I thought. I will have to ask Nash how long they have been friends.

"Who won that round?" I asked the guys.

Jake looks at Nash laughing, "I did, Nash wishes he could win once."

"Oh, I will." Nash snapped.

I gently laugh, "Are you guys ready to go?"

"Yeah." He walks back to the cars. I get into Nash's. I watch Jake get into his fox body.

I look at Nash, "Fox body style is so ugly."

"His is so fast, I wouldn't even mind driving his once." He said.

We get stopped at a red light. Jake pulls up next to us. They roll down the windows. "Wanna race again?"

"Hell yeah," Nash grins back.

"Kallie would you be okay with that?"

"Yea I guess." My voice is shaking.

The light turns green they both go. Suddenly a cop pulls behind Jake. Nash takes a turn to avoid getting caught by the cops. Jake kept going.

"Do you think he got a ticket?" I asked.

"Oh yeah, he did. No way he could take his way out of that." Nash smirked.

I look at the floorboard. "I am glad it wasn't you."

We meet back up with Jake at another red light. "I got a ticket."

Nash is laughing gently. "I figured when you kept going straight and didn't try to avoid them."

"I am going home. You and Kallie be safe. There is a lot of cops out."

"Will do."

We get back to Nash's house. I sit on the couch. "Today was a lot of fun." I never would have guessed I like drag racing.

"Yeah, it is fun, but it is an expensive hobby."

"Do you usually race on the streets too?"

"No, I just know that road and no one ever takes it." He looks at me. "Cops are never on that street."

I need to change the subject. "I need to go let Maverick out."

"You can bring him here. I like Maverick."

I quickly leave to go get Maverick. He runs straight to Nash.

"I think my dog really likes you."

He chuckles, "It's all the treats I give him."

I let Maverick out in Nash's back yard. He runs straight for the sunny corner in the back. I go back to Nash.

"I have a lot of studying to do tomorrow." I sigh.

"I am working long hours tomorrow." Nash's voice went flat.

"Oh ok." I nod.

I let Maverick back inside. He goes to lay in front of the fireplace. He went straight for the blanket next to the fireplace. I watch Maverick dig a hole for him to lay in.

"That is his favorite spot in the house." I smile at Nash,

"Only because your couch has too many people on it for him to fit." I said as Nash laughs.

I am exhausted from today's events. Nash is watching tv. We both fall asleep on the couch.

8

Nash

I hate Holden. I love Kallie. The closer I get to Kallie, the more she is starting to see the jealous side of me.

The closer I get to her; I can tell I hurt her more and more. It's not intentional. I just get this feeling washing over me that causes me to do crazy thing.

I hate how Holden gets to spend every moment with Kallie that I can't. I saw the way he was looking at her today. That wasn't just a friend look. It's obvious Holden wants more than Kallie does. I don't even know how she doesn't see that.

I hate how Kallie thinks I am being unreasonable. I just wish I could tell her how much I love her. I wish she could see she is everything I think about. I wish she knew exactly how I feel. It's hard for me to tell her. I don't want her to think I am damaged. I never will tell her about Emma. I never want Kallie to think less of me. Even if I do push her away.

I saw the way Holden looked at Kallie. It made me infuriated. I felt my eyes burning from the rage. I wanted to go to Kallie's party. I couldn't I knew Holden would be there. I had to go see Emma. She gave me a choice. Either Kallie or my son. I picked my son.

Jake comes over sitting outside. "Do you think I should tell Kallie about my son and Emma?" I watch Jake rub his chin. I had the sounds he makes while doing it. "Yeah, you may even feel better. Stop carrying that around with you." I throw my cigarette down. "How?" "Man, I don't know, but you better tell her soon before she finds out on her own." Jake would never tell Kallie about it.

We walk back into the garage. I look around at the mess. I roll my eyes in annoyance. I need to put them back into the toolbox.

Kallie approaches the garage, making Jake jump.

"Can I come in?"

"Of course."

I walk towards her giving her a kiss. I feel her pulling on my sweatshirt pulling me closer. I put some distance between us when I realize Jake is still sitting there.

"I am just going to leave."

I nod to Jake, and he smiles at Kallie. I roll my eyes.

I sit down on the stool behind her. I pull her closer to me, kissing the side of her neck. I can hear a sharp intake. She turns to face me, wrapping her arms around my neck. I pick her up and carry her upstairs to my bedroom. Two flights of stairs are rough with her kissing my neck. I squeeze her thighs as I carry her up the last steps. I place her on my bed. She starts lifting my shirt over my head. I unbutton my jeans and slide out of them. I look at her and take off her shirt and jeans. I take a step back, admiring her body. I am so hard. I start kissing her ankles up to her thighs. I creep to the inside of her thighs. She places her feet on my back, nudging me towards her center. I listen to her request. I start to lick and bite her. I hear her gasping for air as soon as my tongue hits her center. Her breathing starts to increase. Her feet press deeper into my back as her thighs grips the side of my face. I push up, her eyes meeting mine. "Fuck, you are sexy." I kiss her throat, making my way to meet her mouth. I slide inside her. She is dripping and too tight. I start pushing harder into her. I follow her moans.

"Say my name."

"Nash," she whimpers.

I feel her reach to the edge. I explode inside of her. I roll next to her, trying to catch my breath. I watch her leave to go clean up. I steady my breathing while waiting for her.

"That was amazing."

"You haven't seen anything yet."

She climbs into my bed beside me. She places her hand on my chest, grinding her hand up and down. This girl has no idea what a single touch from her does to me.

"Are you still upset with me?"

"No, but you can't be jealous of Holden. We have talked about this several times now. He is my best friend."

"Should I worry about Jake?"

She sits up, looking at me. "No, Jake is my friend, but he is also your best friend. I would never do that."

I know she would never do that, but that doesn't mean he wouldn't try anything. He knows too much about me. Well, he knows everything about me and how I got to be the way I am. He knows better than to cross me. I will fuck him up.

She lays back down on my chest listening to my heartbeat. I know it will not be long before she falls asleep. I place my hand on her back holding her tightly. These are the moments I never want to leave her. I am so happy I work in the morning and not tonight.

I take in her scent, soft like vanilla. It smells incredible on her. Her breathing as slowed; I am almost positive she is sleeping. I kissed her on her head. I make sure she is good asleep.

"I love you Kallie," I whisper into her ear.

I feel her body press deeper into mine. Tonight, I can go to bed happy.

Today, we are supposed to go to the rodeo. I am nervous because it is one of the most popular things to do around here. I get dressed in a flannel and jeans. I head to Kallie's house.

I knocked on the door, I can hear Maverick barking so I know she is already dressed. She opens the door quickly. Wow she looks amazing in pink flannel and ripped jeans. I pull my eyes back up to hers, I lean in for a kiss.

"Come in, it's still snowing."

I walk in and Maverick instantly starts wanting to play.

"Are you almost ready?"

"Yeah, I just gotta grab my coffee."

I watch her pour her coffee and make me a cup. She comes back with a smile while she hands me my cup. I take a sip before we leave.

I can tell she is so cold. Her body is shaking, I wish I brought a jacket for her. I lean in closer enveloping my arms around her. She lays her head into my shoulder as we wait in the ticket line. God, I love this girl. I could hold her forever.

We make our way through the building after scanning our tickets. We find our seats I offer to find her coffee but she says she is fine. I wrap my arm around her.

she watches the horses. By the time the bulls comes she looks uncomfortable. I assure her the bulls are not actually hurt and she relaxes a little.

I scan the people around us, I spot Jake and Bree. I give him a smirk. I don't know what he's doing but whatever. I relax a little knowing Kallie is with me. I have her full attention.

While she is watching the rodeo, I can't help but to look at her. She is so breath taking and all mine. I shift my focus from her to the rodeo, as I hear her gasp and cover her face. Shit, the rider is all bloody from being trampled.

"Kallie are you ok?"

"Yeah the blood isn't that bad."

I forget that blood makes me queasy. I pull her closer into me. She grips my shirt pulling me closer to her. Her big blue eyes are staring up at mine.

"Your hazel eyes are so beautiful."

I chuckle out, "thank you."

I place my hand on the side of her face while I lean in for a kiss. I get lost in the moment as our tongues swirl around together. Dancing absently together. I hear a soft moan from her as I pull away.

"Sorry," she mumbles.

"Don't apologize for kissing me. I could kiss you all day every day."

She sits there, eyes locked on mine, "Are you ready to go?"

I grab her by the hand and lead her out to my truck. i start the engine to heat up the truck. I see her playing with the holes in her jeans.

"Are you ok?"

"Yeah."

Right. She is never this quiet.

"Well do you wanna go back to my house?"

I see her nod in agreement, I drive to my house as the tension builds.

I pull into the driveway, Kallie is still as quiet as can be.

"What's on your mind?"

"You."

I lead her by the hand. I sit on my couch waiting for her to join me. I hear the shower starting. I pad in there to see what she is doing. I see her standing there with her shirt unbuttoned. She slides it off and I move behind her kissing her neck down to her shoulders. She turns around and starts to unbutton mine and sliding it off of me. Kallie slides down my pants and quickly takes her off before getting into the shower.

I stand behind her, waiting for her to say anything. I pull her closer so she can feel me growing up on her back. My arms wrap around her chest.

"I want you now."

I slide my hand down her stomach and start playing with her clit. She lets a moan slip from her mouth. I can feel her legs start to tremble. She turns around and gets on her knees, taking my whole length.

"Kallie," I let out a deep moan.

She swallows me whole. I am almost to the point of letting go. I guide her up and press her hands into the wall, taking her from behind. I thrust my hips into her. I can hear her whimpering. Her whole body starts shaking while she breathes harder and harder. She collapse in my arms. I pick her up and begin to wash her body, kissing all her sensitive parts.

She slowly turns to face me, cupping her hands over my face.

"Nash, I love you so much, but you have to stop being so back and forth."

"What do you mean?"

"The hot and cold."

I nod in agreement, "I will."

I wish she could see how good I try to be for her. I try to be everything she needs and wants. I will also burn the world for her.

We dry off and I lay with her before I have to go to work. I really don't want to leave her. I see the clock telling me that I need to leave before I am late. I grab my shoes and jacket from the front door. I sneak out without waking her up.

9

Kallie

I wake up to banging on the front door. I stumble my way from Nash's couch. I open the door with a confused look on my face.

"Nash is at work, Jake." I tell Jake.

"He was supposed to help me with my car today."

"I am sure you can use his garage." I watch Jake turn to walk to the garage.

Jake stops walking and turns to me. "Kallie, can you move the Mustang out of the garage?"

"Yeah, I can." I grab the keys from the entry table.

"Do you know how to drive a manual?"

"Yeah, my dad taught me in case I ever need to know it." I start to back out of the garage. I knew the car had power; it is significantly more than I was expecting. I slowly back it out. I park it in my driveway.

I take Maverick outside to play fetch. "Kallie, Can I get a glass of water?"

"Yeah, I will make it for you." I go to the kitchen to make Jake ice water.

"Here is my number, if you need anything just text or call me."

"Thanks that would be a huge help. Any chance you know how to work on cars?"

I laugh, "Absolutely not Jake."

Jake comes back inside. Jake is finally done with his car. "I am leaving now. Tell Nash thanks for letting me use his tools." I nod. I need to text Nash that came was here fixing the car. I grab my phone. Jake was here fixing his car. Nash: Ok did he leave. Me: Yes, I wasn't sure if you knew. I wait for Nash to text back. I guess he is busy.

I need to fill out my graduation packets. Holden keeps asking if I submitted it yet. As I am filling out the papers, it really starts to seem real. I graduate in a next month. I still have no idea what I am going to do after college. The thought is terrifying.

I hear my phone vibrating on the counter. "Hello?" I answer.

"Hey Kallie. Would you like to go get ice cream with me?

"Yeah sure. I will meet you there in about 20 minutes?"

"Ok see you soon." Jake hangs up.

On my drive there I feel nervous. Jake never asks to hang out with just me. I arrived after him.

"What do you want to order?"

"I will take a Reese's ice cream."

Of course, Jake would pay for me.

"You really don't have to pay for me Jake. I am a paid intern."

He smiles at me I see his dimples I have never noticed before. His smile is contagious. I can see why Bree is so protective of him.

"Let us go sit over here. It is in the sun."

"Yeah, the sun does feel nice. Spring is still a little chilly." I say, looking at him.

"Where is Bree?"

"She didn't want to come." I nod. I do not know how to respond to that.

"Kallie, Can I ask you something?"

I let out a sharp breath, "yeah of course you can."

"Why are you with Nash? He does not treat you right. You deserve someone that is not him"

My mind is racing. What does Jake mean by he does not treat me right? I take a panic gasp.

"What are you trying to tell me?"

"Well, did you know he has a son?"

Oh, here it comes. All the trust I had in Nash could be gone in seconds. Jake has no reason to lie to me. As I shake my head,

"No I didn't know." I pause. "He does not tell me anything about his past. Only his present and future."

"You never thought why?"

"No Jake, I didn't." I take a long pause. "We were at Coffee, and Books I saw this girl staring us down with a toddler. I did not think anything of it."

Now it makes sense why that girl was staring. She never spoke to either of us.

I suddenly do not want my ice cream. My head is spinning, and it is out of control. If Nash can keep that a secret what else can be a secret.

"Kallie, you, ok?" Jake looks concerned.

I cannot tell him no. I half smile, "yeah, I am fine."

"Want to take Maverick and my dog, Marlee, to the dog park?"

"Yes, I do."

I do not mind. Maverick and Marlee enjoying playing together. Holden and Jake are my only friends really. I am almost positive Jake is only friends with me because I am with Nash.

We leave to go get out dogs. I almost ran a red light I am so distracted from the news I just found out. I am shocked to know he has a son. That is a huge secret to keep. Why wouldn't he just tell me. I have more questions than answers now. I park next to Jake's truck at the park.

I watch as Jake throws the tennis ball to the dogs.

"You know when Bree and I broke up it hurt. It took me a little while to see she was right."

"What do you mean?"

"She said we were growing apart and wanted different things in life. I thought it was bullshit. The more I reflected on it the more I realized she was right about it."

I turn to face him, "I did not know there was a breakup. I just thought she did not want to be in the middle of Nash and I and you felt guilty."

"I was feeling guilty, the more I got to know you the more I knew you had no idea what type of guy he really is."

"You are not wrong. I just never knew I could love someone so much. I know what people say about him; they say it about all of us."

Jake turns his head with smile almost laughing. "Nash is different from the rest of us. Even Willow has her own issues with Nash.

"Are you friend with Willow?"

"Yes, but we rarely talk about Nash."

"Kallie, you do realize Nash bought coffee and books for her. He owns the business, she manages it."

"Jake are you serious? He told me it was her dream to own a coffee shop, so she worked to make it happen."

"Yeah, he can be humble sometimes." Jake called Marlee to him, Maverick is close behind, it is almost sunset. I do need to go home.

"Do you want to come with Marlee and me?"

"No, I need to go home, I am almost positive Nash is wondering where I am."

I get maverick in the car, of course he picks the passenger seat. he loves to look out the window. I spent the day with Jake. I feel a little guilty for not telling Nash where I will be. He gets so jealous, if he knew I was with Jake, he would literally lose it. "Almost home buddy," I tell maverick. I open the car door. Maverick goes straight to the door. I wipe his paws and head to my bedroom. I have no idea what to think or feel about this current information.

Nash text me: Can you come outside?

Me: Give me a second.

I grab my shoes.

"Hey, why are we outside?"

"Why were you with Jake today?"

"How do you know I was with Jake? I look down at my feet.

I wait for him to respond and he doesn't.

"We went for ice cream and took our dogs to the park. I didn't think it would be a big deal because he is your friend."

He looks so frustrated. "I don't like it when you hang out with my friends without me."

I cross my arms, "Jake is my friend too."

"Stay away from him Kallie!"

I do not like his tone. I turn to walk away; he cannot control me. "Kallie, wait!" He grabs my wrist, "I am sorry, please don't walk away."

"Nash have you been drinking?" I can smell liquor on his breath.

"Yeah, we live next to a bar. Jake told me he was with you today. Did anything happen?"

"No, of course not. Why would you even think that?"

"I know him, you don't!" Nash shouts.

I roll my eyes. "Do you have a son?"

"What! where is this coming from?"

"I saw how that girl was looking at you at the coffee shop. The boy with her looks like you."

"No, I don't have any kids." He pulls me closer. "I told you; I don't want kids."

I am so angry with Nash. I don't know if I even want to be his close to him. Nash is lying to my face or either Jake is. I want to believe Nash, but something is telling me to believe Jake.

Nash wraps his arms around my back. I sigh, I don't want him touching me I am so upset. I try to move away. He grabs my arm, "Stop."

"Kallie please"

"What— what do you want Nash?

"Please say you will not see Jake again without me."

"Fine." I sigh.

He starts running his fingers through my hair. I look up at him; He looks upset as much as I am. I really do not like being told what to do. I also feel like Nash has valid reasons to ask this from me.

"Promise you will work on your jealously?"

"I will try."

I follow him back to his deck. I sit down and look up at the stars. "It really is a beautiful night."

"Yes, it is." I take a deep breath in.

The stars are beautiful when there is not any light pollution. This is exactly why I live in this small town. I see out of the corner of my eye Nash is looking at me.

"What are you thinking?"

Nash half smiles, "I'm thinking about how beautiful you are."

I start to blush. "Oh, yeah?" I really hate being so awkward.

I go back to my house. I start to wonder if Jake is telling me the truth. He has no reason to lie to me. If Nash is lying to me, that is a problem. I understand he doesn't want kids, but if it is his kid, he should not deny the child. I feel even more confused than I did earlier. Nash knows I don't like being lied too. I want to believe Nash is a good person. He hasn't done anything to make me think anything differently. He does get jealous, but I feel it's only because he doesn't want me to leave.

I decided to call Holden. "I need to talk to you about Nash?"

"Are you ok Kallie?"

"No, Nash and I had a fight. I was with Jake today, which made Nash angry. Jake told me that Nash does have a son. Nash is telling me he doesn't. He is jealous of every guy friend I have. I just don't know what to do."

I hear Holden take a deep breath. "Well, you are in a relationship with Nash not Jake. I would listen to Jake, but I would believe Nash. I am not sure if Jake is telling the truth. Have you thought if Jake wants to break you guys up?"

"No Jake is Nash's best friend. We have started to form a friendship, but we are not close."

"Kallie, take a deep breath, it's going to be ok. You and Nash had a fight. All couples fight. You do need to talk about his jealously."

"Yeah, I told him he has no reason to be jealous of you or Jake. I explained how we are friends."

"So, it should be ok. Maybe he has trust issues because other girls before you did him wrong."

"I guess but he shouldn't take it out on me."

"No, but damage is damage. It just may take longer for him to trust."

"Thanks Holden. I am going to go shower and sleep. Today was rough."

"Ok, call me if you need anything else."

I hang up with Holden. All I gathered was Nash may have trust issues because of his past. We all have issues from out pass, unless you are really lucky. Nash isn't planning on opening up anytime soon. I almost feel like Nash is trying to push me away.

The next morning, I noticed Nash is standing outside. I debate if I want to be late for class. I do. I walk towards Nash; he is staring me down.

"Hey Nash." I lean to give him a kiss.

"Kallie, I am no good for you. You need someone better."

I cross my arms. "Nash, where is this coming from? If you want space, I can give you space."

Nash crosses his arm, matching my body language. "Kallie, I don't even know." I stare at him.

Well, I am going to class. You need to figure it out." I walk past him in a hurry. He doesn't get to see me upset. He needs to figure out what he wants, not me.

I drive to class, I find Holden. "Nash, told me he isn't good for me, and I need someone better." He looks puzzled.

"Why? Did you ask questions."

"No, I left to come to class."

Holden pauses, "I think it his way of pushing you away."

I sigh, "Can we talk about this after class?"

We walk to our cars. "Holden, what do I do about Nash?"

"Honestly, Kallie, I think you need to talk to him. I can only give you advice. I think you should tell him how you feel."

"I don't even know how I feel anymore. I am mentally exhausted from all the back and forth."

Holden gives me a tight hug. "You don't have to do anything you do want to do."

At home, I notice Nash is gone. I thought he was working nights this week. I hate how his schedule is always switching. "Maverick, I am back." He growls. "Wake up lets go outside." I open the back door. I throw a tennis ball at Maverick. I watch him bring it back. I start to tell Maverick how I am feeling. He looks over to the fence, Nash is standing there.

"Can we talk Kallie?"

I do not like how he is saying my name. It sounds different.

"Kallie, I am sorry about this morning."I had a rough night and took it out on you."

I take a deep breath. "I thought you were still upset about the fight we had. I didn't know what I did."

"No, it isn't you." I look down at Maverick. "I need to take him back inside."

"I need to go to work."

So, he is working nights.

The back and forth is making my head hurt. One minute he can't wait to see me. Then he acts like he can't stand me. I try my best to avoid him. I sneak into my own house; I look out the window before I dash to my car. I need to focus on work. I need a full-time job after graduation. I pull out my laptop to order my cap, gown, and honor cords. I am grateful Holden will be with me during graduation. I pour myself a glass of wine. I can't believe I am graduating with honors. I sip on my wine while reflecting on my college years. I didn't party much, spent way too much time alone or with Holden. I am still not ready to graduate. I know I will miss classes and my internship.

The moonlight is still shining through my bedroom windows. I hear Maverick huff downstairs. Nash walks into my bedroom, sits down in the chair.

"Kallie, you awake?"

"Mhm, you know it's still night out?"

"It's actually 4 am."

"What do you need Nash?" I open my eyes; I look at him.

"I don't want to do this back and forth with you."

"This could wait until morning." I say as I pull the blankets over my head.

"No, just listen. I— I need to be with you. You make me a better person; I wake up thinking about you. I go to bed thinking about you. You are my everything Kallie. I need you in my life. I know I mess up a lot. I am trying to change that for you."

I pull my blankets back motioning him to get in with me. I place my head on his chest, "Nash, I love you, but you cannot keep doing this to me. Its absolute hell without you." He kisses my forehead.

"I love you; I promise I will do better."

The sun was shining brightly in the windows. I check the time. 6:30. I try to escape from Nash's arm. I feel him moving.

"Don't go."

"I have to go to class for finals. I will be back as soon as I can."

For May it is still a little chilly outside. I slip on my ripped jeans, a shirt and my cardigan. I get dressed quickly as I can. I stopped by Coffee and Books for Holden and me.

"Kallie, I need to talk with you. Are you busy?" Willow asks.

"Can I call you after class? I have finals today."

I rush to class with coffee in hand for Holden. I walk with him while he sips on his coffee, I read the flash cards and of course he doesn't miss one answer.

"Are you ready for the final exam?" Holden glances at me.

"Yeah, I think so. I studied really hard." I said.

Holden laughs, "I am sure you did." I side eye him.

After the exam, I search for Holden. I find him waiting on me at my car.

"That wasn't as hard as I expected it to be."

"Nothing is hard if you actually studied."

After the final is over, I call Willow. "I need to speak with you about Nash."

"What is it?"

"I know it hasn't been easy. He has a lot of held on anger from our parents. He was them happy one day to our dad walking out with no notice. He believes he will never get his happy ending. You make him happy. I've never seen him like this. Please be patient with him."

I kind of figured something happened to make him like this. I hang up with Willow. It hurts hearing that from her, when Nash should have been the one to tell me this. I knew a little about his past from small talk with him and Willow. We are not his parents. We are Nash and Kallie; we are different people.

10

Nash

Why is Kallie questioning me about a son? Did Emma contact her? Did Emma tell her I was abusive?

Emma told me it wasn't my son. I believed her. I saw him today. He looks like me when I was younger. It's been three years since I've seen Emma. I moved out of the city to avoid ever seeing her.

I never abused Emma. She liked being slapped during sex. She always demanded it harder. Her friend saw bruises on her body and her red face. I guess she decided to take the easy way out. The news of me being an abuser traveled around quickly. I stopped dating completely. No one ever looked at me the same. I don't blame them. I do not stand for any time of violence.

Emma almost ruined my career.

When Jake told me he was with Kallie today, I got jealous. I just want her to stay away from him when I am not there. I know Jake wouldn't do anything to hurt her, but would she be tempted to leave me? Jake is a better fit for Kallie as well. He is tall with a wonderful career. I have a suitable career. I bought Willow a coffee shop she always dreamed of owning. I didn't want Kallie to know about that. I save more than I spend. I never want my family to feel like I did when I was a teenager.

I trust Kallie. It is hard to fully trust her. I fully trusted Emma. She little by little destroyed me emotionally. I want to be able to tell Kallie everything. Maybe even explain why I am the way I am. She wouldn't understand. No one ever understand until it happens to them.

Jake just walks inside and slides on my counter, "I need something strong."

I scrunch my face and grab two glasses and a bottle of whiskey.

"You look rough."

"Well Bree said I'm not what she is looking for and decided to end it," he said while using his fingers as air quotes.

"Well shit. I thought you guys would be end game," I said while pouring us a glass.

"Me too."

I hand him his drink and he takes it in one gulp.

If Bree and Jake can't make things work, how the hell are the rest of us supposed to make anything work? We don't. Bree does put up with a lot of his shit. I give it to her for putting up with him this long.

I pour him another glass as he slams it down.

"Ya know, this isn't a bar."

"Close enough."

I nod. I'm not one to be good at comforting people, much less a man that just got his heartbroken.

"Nash, don't ever fall in love. It's terrible."

"Too late."

He eyes me while processing the information. I know I have fucked up a lot but it's only because I don't want to lose her. The thought of it scares the shit out of me but also because I don't— no can't — see her hurt because of me and my games. I just don't know how to be the man she needs.

11

I go back home and to my surprise; he was already cooking my favorite pasta. I do not lock my back door, so I knew he would just let himself in.

"Hey love." Nash said as he walked behind me.

I take a moment and just look at him. "

"I love it when you call me love."

"It is because I love you."

I climb on to the counter like I usually do when he is cooking.

"Want a drink?" Nash asked.

" I sure do. It has been a long day." He grabs me by a bud light and kisses me. Dinner is almost done, and it smells incredible.

Nash has work tonight, so he left after dinner. I clean up my kitchen. I decided to call Holden.

"Hey, Nash left, so I wanted to talk."

"They posted grades from the final. Have you looked yet?"

"Already? No, I have not. I thought it would be a few days. I am cleaning my kitchen. Then I will check."

"I passed with a 98," Holden tells me.

"I am not surprised. You are really smart. I will text you once I check it out." I clean as fast as I can. I run upstairs. I check my grade. I text Holden: I got a 94. Holden: I am impressed. Me: Same.

I throw my phone beside me in bed. I grab the remote to watch tv. There is nothing on. I put on a science fiction tv show. I didn't realize how exhausted I was.

Mavericks' aggressive barking wakes me up. He rarely barks at night. I hear movement outside. I quickly run downstairs. I watch from the kitchen window. It is Willow. She looks visibly upset and crying. Nash is walking her back to my house with her.

"Willow, what is wrong?" I asked.

"My boyfriend was cheating on me and just kicked me out. Nash is pretty upset with this situation." I can hear the pain in her voice.

I tell Willow she can stay with me, while Nash goes gets her stuff.

I am sitting with Willow while we wait for Nash to arrive at home. I make her some tea with fresh chamomile and lavender from my garden. It seems like hours pass. Willow falls asleep on my couch. I grab her a blanket and leave her. Nash finally arrives back at his house. I quietly go over there. His lip is bleeding, and his knuckles are bloody.

"Nash, what happened?" I said anxiously.

"He deserved it." He is coldly staring back at me. I help him clean off the blood on his lip. He snaps at me, "That hurts! Stop!"

"No, I need to clean the blood off. I am trying to help you, Nash."

"I do not need help! Fine, I am leaving."

And now, I suddenly hate living next door to Nash. Is this what Jake tried to warn me about? He has never been so angry with me or snapped at me. He does not have to be so rude; I was only trying to help. I look at the clock. It is three am. I am going to bed. I will deal with him in the morning.

When I woke, I saw a text on my phone. I'm sorry for how I acted. Really, a text. I do not respond. He should at least apologize to my face. I go downstairs. Willow was already awake and sitting quietly at the table.

"I made coffee." Willow motions to the kitchen.

"Oh, thanks Willow. I was not expecting you to be awake. Have you seen Nash this morning?" I asked.

"No, I have not. I doubt he even awake," she looks at me. "I am glad Nash has someone like you."

If she only knew what happened last night. I nod my head. I go back to my room. I need to get dressed.

I hear a movement. I turn around and Nash is standing right behind me. "Nash, why are you here? You cannot just come in whenever you feel like it. You really hurt my feelings last night. I was only trying to help you. You are so important to me, but I refuse to be your punching bag. You need help, Nash. Tomorrow is my college graduation. I want you there, but Jake is also coming."

"Ok, I will be there. I promise and on my best behavior." Nash pauses for a moment. "Is Holden coming?"

"Yes, he's graduating as well."

The look of rage on his face says everything I needed to know. He storms out, slamming my door behind him. If he is already acting like this, I don't even want him to come… I can't even convince myself I don't want him there.

I do not want to go to work. I found out Holden was asked to go to South Carolina. I don't want my best friend to leave. I sit down at my desk. There is an envelope with my name on it. I look at Holden.

"I got a letter asking if I could go too!" I try to contain my excitement. This is huge for my career. I never thought they would offer me a position. "We need to celebrate!"

I am exhausted after work. I need coffee, I go to Books and Coffee. Willow is working.

"Hey, can you come over when you get off?"

Willow smiles. "I am actually off in 10 minutes. I can come by."

I will receive my order. I go home. Willow quickly is at my door. I let her in.

"Hey Kallie," Maverick comes running to Willow. She pets maverick's head, "Hey Maverick."

"I wanted to talk about your brother."

"I figured."

Willow takes a deep breath. "He has his issues. We all do. Nash is difficult."

"Can you tell me more?" I walk to the couch.

"He had this girlfriend. She completely broke him emotionally. Now he has trust issues, and jealously issues. Before her, he was gentle and kind now. He is rough around the edges."

I cross my arms. "What about a child?"

Willow smiles. "She told him it isn't his child. It obviously is, she refuses to even talk to Nash anymore."

"So, he doesn't even really know it's his son?"

"Nope, he wanted to get an attorney to find out the truth. So far, he isn't having much luck to find anyone to take the case."

I nod. "I wish he would have told me. That is a huge secret to keep."

Willow looks at the time. "I do have to go." I nod.

I hear my doorbell, which is odd. Nash never uses the doorbell. I let him inside.

"Hey. Are you ok?" I asked Nash.

"I am just tired. I wanted to see you."

"Don't forget my graduation is tomorrow night."

"I remembered; I am working then coming straight to it."

He lays down on my couch. I grab the tv remote and lay next to him. I find a series to watch.

I wake up to Nash's alarm. We slept on the couch all night.

"Nash, your alarm is going off."

"I have to go get ready for work."

He gives me a kiss and leaves. Now I get to relax before my big day. I should text Holden to see when he is getting there tonight.

Me: What time are you getting there tonight?

Holden: I plan on leaving at 5:30 to make it by 6.

I'm getting dressed. I decided on my favorite black lace dress, black tights and black lace heels. You really can't go wrong with black. I feel like I look amazing. I grab my cap and gown and find my keys and phone. I have a message from Nash: be about 10 minutes late. Love you and proud of you. I take a deep breath, not wanting to look disappointed. I have to leave, or I will be late.

It's finally time for my graduation. Nash promised he would be here. I do not see him anywhere. I find Holden.

"Is Nash here?" Holden asked.

"I have not seen him yet. He said he would be 10 minutes late."

I am listening to all the names being called. Holden nudges me. Of course, Nash shows up an hour late.

"Did he know what time it started?" Holden whispers as he leans over.

"Yes, and I told him how important this is to me."

At least he showed up. My heart felt like it dropped to my stomach. I try
not to look angry or disappointed. I walked before Holden. We made it back to our seats. It was the moment I've been waiting for. I throw my cap in the air; I catch it.

I look at Holden. "Let's take a photo." He snaps a few photos of us with and without our caps on.

"I am going to find Nash. Wanna meet me at the front doors?" He nods.

I rush through the crowd to find Nash.

"Why are you so late?"

"I had to work and shower."

"Right, so ten minutes late turned into an hour?"

A moment passed without him saying anything. I try to control my anger.

"Let's take photos, then we can leave."

Holden takes photos of us. Nash takes photos of Holden and me.

"I will meet you back at my house, Nash?"

"Yeah, sure."

"Holden, do you want to come over and celebrate?"

"Do you think it will be weird?"

"No, I don't. I think it will be fun."

I arrive at my house first. I run upstairs and change quickly. I pull my phone out of my jacket. A missed call and text from Nash. Something came up. I can't make It tonight. What the hell came up that is more important than me. I am so upset, and heart broken. I have noticed he is acting weird lately. Holden is knocking on my bedroom door.

"Can I come in?"

"Sure."

"Your college graduation is supposed to be a night to remember. If he wanted to be here, he would be."

"Holden, you are not wrong."

Holden takes a long pause before speaking. "Can I ask you something?"

"Of course you can."

"Kallie, do you love him?"

"Well, yeah, he just hurt me, and I don't know if I can be ok with that." I take a long breath before I can even finish my thought. "Some days, things are really good, and others aren't. He tries so hard to be the man I need him to be."

Holden pulls me in for a hug. "I know. Do you want me to stay here tonight? We can celebrate together."

"It is our night." I said.

Holden and I go to the kitchen. I grab two wine glasses from the cabinet. "Oh Kallie, we just graduated from college with honors. This deserves more than wine. I brought our favorite whiskey and soda."

"You are so right Holden!"

I hear my phone text alert go off. It is Nash, Hey. Can we talk? I stare at my phone thinking of a reply. I don't want to reply but I know I should.

"Are you ok?"

"No, Nash just texted me. I don't have anything to say to him." I left him on read.

"You can deal with him in the morning."

"You really should leave him alone. He isn't good for you. I never see you smile anymore."

"I know. It's hard. Even if I push him away, he keeps coming back."

Holden passes me another drink. "cheers" we both say.

I turn on the music. Holden starts dancing. I laugh so hard, watching him, trying to twirl like a ballerina.

"Holden, who taught you how to dance?"

He nuzzles my arm. "Shut up Kallie, at least I am trying."

I do a double pirouette. "This is how you do it."

He almost spills his drink from giggling. "Not everyone was a ballerina."

"Yeah, I know. Maybe I can give you a lesson." I wink at Holden.

Having fun with Holden is a different fun. He accepts my weirdness. Soon we both will be in South Carolina doing what we love.

"Cheers to a fun future together!" I clink my cup with Holden's. He spilled a little and I start to giggle.

"I think I had enough. I can't feel my face anymore."

Let's go watch TV. Holden falls asleep on my couch. I cover Holden up with a blanket from my couch. I whisper, "Good night, Holden." I walk up the stairs to my bedroom.

I feel like I didn't even sleep. I should go downstairs to make coffee. I put my favorite cardigan on. It feels so cold in my house. I make my way to the kitchen. Holden is still asleep on the couch. I walk into my kitchen until I see Nash's truck in the driveway. I turn on the faucet to fill up my carafe. I pour the water in the coffeemaker. I made it extra strong this morning. I need all the caffeine I can get. I grab two mugs out of the cabinet. I make Holden and I coffee.

I gently wake up Holden. "Hey, I made coffee."

"Extra strong?"

"Yes, with cream, no sugar."

"Perfect." Holden's voice is still sleepy.

"Do you also need water?"

"No, not yet. Thanks for asking."

I think Saturday is going to be a lazy day. Holden looks at me. "Any plans today?"

"I need to clean up a bit and stuff around the house."

"Do you want help? I did help make the mess."

"No, it is fine. I can do it. It will keep me busy."

I am finding out so much information lately. I am angry and confused. Nash completely blew off my college graduation. He wants to know if that is his son. He still refuses to tell me about any of this. Maybe I should avoid him for a few days. It will be difficult since I live next door to him. I will try my hardest to be focused on my internship.

I feel so alone. I decided to watch the sunset from my roof. I love to watch the sunset just behind the trees. My phone keeps vibrating. Hey. Another one comes Kallie; I can see you on the roof. Stop avoiding me. It really irritates me. He will not leave me alone. Suddenly, I hear someone coming through the window to the roof.

"What do you want, Nash? Do you enjoy seeing me sad?"

He pauses way too long. "No, I don't like seeing you sad at all."

"All you have done lately has hurt me. I ask you to come to one event that is important to me. You acted like I was an inconvenience."

I watch as Nash moves behind me. He gently pulls me closer to him. I tense up.

"Please let me make it up to you."

"No, you have shown me I am not important to you." My voice is stern and tired.

"I will never stop trying for you."

I feel like I should believe him despite what Holden and Jake are telling me. "Nash, I have plans tonight. You should leave."

"With whom?"

"That is none of your business anymore."
I snap.

I am having a party at my house to celebrate Holden and I promotion. Holden arrives first.

"Hey Kallie, where do you want me to put the beer?"

"Kitchen counter please, and can you let Maverick outside?" I run down the stairs.

"Hey Kallie, Sorry I let myself in."

"It is fine Jake."

"Do you think Nash is going to crash it?"

"I don't think so. I told him I had plans tonight. He will see Holden's car."

Holden joins Jake and me in the kitchen.

Jake looks at me, half smiling, "When does everyone leave for South Carolina?"

Holden speaks first. "I leave in a few weeks."

"I am not completely sure when I am leaving. I still have to talk to my boss about dates. I also need to list my house for sale."

Jake is frowning. "I am going to miss you, Kallie."

"I know. It is a great opportunity for me."

Holden chuckles. "Anyone want to play a card game?"

Jake and Holden glance at me.

"Drinking 21" I suggest.

Holden sighs. "Okay."

We sit down to play. My phone is vibrating the whole table.

"Let me guess. Nash is calling?" Holden said with a puzzle look on his face.

"Probably. I just want to enjoy my time with you guys." I watch as Jake deals.

"I am going to put my phone in the living room to play music in the background.

I must be lucky tonight. I keep winning. I watch as Holden takes another shot.

"I think I need a break. I will deal. Jake, you're up against Kallie."

My lucky strike is coming to an end with Jake. We are shot for shot now. It is getting harder to count. Jake laughs. "I think I need to stop playing this game."

"I agree." I said.

Holden stands up. "I am going to get going."

"Are you ok to drive?" I asked.

"Yes, it has been hours since I had anything except water." I walk Holden to the front door. I hug him goodbye.

"I should be leaving too." Jake said.

"No, Jake, you can stay here. I have plenty of room."

"What about Nash?"

"I will deal with him later. I am still very angry with him."

"Oh, another fight?"

"I don't think he can come back from this one."

He looks at me like he wants to speak. "I said I wouldn't get in the middle. I am both of your friends. So, if it is me, I can talk to him. He has no reason not to trust us together."

"No, it's because of my graduation. He was an hour late and something came up, so he couldn't come celebrate afterward.

"Does he know about South Carolina?"

I suck on my lips. "No, not yet at least."

"Your secret is safe with me."

I help walk Jake up the stairs. I help him to the bedroom across from mine.

"You can stay in this room tonight. I will be across the hall if you need anything."

"Alright." Jake replied.

I grab him a blanket from the closet. "If you need any more blankets, they are in the closet."

I turn off the light as I walk out of the room. I can't help but to look back at Jake one last time before I shut the door. I lay in my bed wondering what am I doing? The drunk thoughts are loud and will not stop. I turn on thunderstorm sounds on my phone; I need to sleep.

12

Nash

I am so angry with Willow's ex-boyfriend. I didn't mean to punch him. I blacked out when he called her a "good-for-nothing slut." I didn't mean to snap at Kallie for cleaning the blood off my face. My lip was hurting badly. I only went to her bedroom the next day to see if she was still angry with me. I needed to apologize.

Kallie doesn't deserve to be hurt my me. I was late for her graduation, nor did I go to her party. I was with Emma. I couldn't tell her what I was doing. I wanted to see my son. Emma finally agreed to let me see him and talk. I've waited three years for this.

Now Kallie is avoiding me. I saw her sitting on the roof. I went to her roof because I knew she couldn't run away. When she looked at me, her face was full of disappointment. I felt like I was dying seeing her like that. I need to push her away. It won't hurt so badly if she is already halfway out the door.

Until she fully understands my life, she will only be more disappointed.

I am proud Kallie got a promotion. It stings a little. She doesn't want me there. I don't blame her. I knew how important graduation was to her and I still didn't go. I am an idiot.

I get home from Emma's and I see Jake's truck. Holden's car is gone. Is Jake staying the night with Kallie? I should go over there. Kallie never locks her door. I could sneak in and out without anyone noticing. Maverick is so used to me he wouldn't bark at me. I push those thoughts out of my head and walk into my house.

I can't believe I ruined the most important day for Kallie. I bet she is lying in bed right now, wondering what the hell even happened. I am sure by now Jake has told her everything. I shouldn't be mad at him. They became friends because of me. I feel the rage creeping up. I want nothing more than to punch that jackass in the face.

I can feel the heat radiating from my body as I walk over there. I let myself in. I head straight for Kallie's room. Relief washes over me when I find her in bed alone. I gently place my hand on her arm.

"Hey Kallie."

"Go away. I don't want to see you."

Ouch, that burns.

"I need to see you and tell you what happened.'

She sits up facing me, "unless the world is burning down, I don't want to hear it."

I lean in closer to her, grabbing her face gently. I pull in closer to her waiting for her to protest. Before she could even open her mouth, mine is landing on hers. I feel her push me away.

"I will scream if you don't leave."

"I just want to tell you what happened and why I was late."

"Let me guess, you had your tongue down another girl's throat."

Ouch double burn.

"It wasn't exactly like that."

Maybe it's better she doesn't know about any of this, and I just leave. I stand and glance down at her.

"One day you will know."

I leave her room and slam the door behind me. I hear Jake rushing to Kallie's room. I can't even believe he is still there and not on the couch. I hate him even more now. I am still so angry and hurt, I don't notice the frosty night is making my lungs burn.

I go straight to my bedroom. I am lucky my room looks into Kallie's windows. I want- no need- to see if Jake goes in there. I keep waiting and wait. I don't see any lights on in her room. I look to see if I can see them downstairs and, of course, at this angle I can't. I storm down to my kitchen that faces Kallie's kitchen. Of course, he is there leaning against the counter while she is sitting on it. I swear if he touches her, I will go back over there. I see him move to her side. I wish I could hear what they are saying. It is killing me just watching them. I scrunch my face in disgust and leave to go back to my room. I have seen enough.

I lay in my bed waiting for any text from her. Hours have passed and I am sure she is already sleep. I check my phone. Nothing. Not even from Jake. of course.

The sun shines right into my window. I am getting even more annoyed. I look out the window. I see Kallie and Maverick. Kallie is looking into her closet. She must be getting ready to go somewhere. Jake's truck is still in the driveway.

I see them walk out together to get in Jake's truck.

What the fuck.

Kallie and I have fights all the time, this one doesn't mean he can move onto my girl. I worked hard to make her love me.

13

This kitchen has so many memories of Nash, it's hard not to think about him. I pour my coffee into my favorite mug. I lean against the kitchen counter while sipping my coffee. I instantly lookout the window. I glance over at Nash's house. His truck is in his driveway. I call for Maverick. He's sleeping under the table. I quietly take Maverick into the backyard. "Hurry up, boy." He takes off to the fence towards Nash's house. I go back inside.

I hear Jake coming from upstairs.

"Thanks for letting me stay here."

I nod.

"Can I get a cup of coffee?" I laugh. I open my cabinet so I can pour Jake a cup.

"Cream or sugar?"

"Just cream please."

I watch Jake drink his coffee. His silence makes me think something is wrong. He places his mug in the sink.

"I should get going before Nash comes over."

"I will walk you out." He leans in for a hug goodbye. I allow my body to press against his while taking in his scent. He smells like vanilla and nutmeg.

I need to clean my kitchen. I start wiping down my counter where I sat my coffee. I start thinking about the first night Nash cooked at my house. I was sitting on this counter smiling and adoring him. I think about the time he first kissed me in the driveway. Maverick barks to let me know he wants back inside. It pulls me from my memories.

I decided to read my favorite novel again. I try to get maverick on the couch to snuggle with. Maverick usually lies on my feet while I read. Saturdays are lazy days.

"After I read a few chapters, I will take you on a run, Maverick." He perks up at me.

I didn't realize hours have passed. I look at Maverick. He is sleeping so I ask him, "Ready to go run?" I quickly change into my running outfit. Slip on my shoes. It is, so it isn't too hot for a run.

It's a quick one mile, then Maverick is ready to go back. Maverick is my favorite running partner because he hates running almost as much as I do. I only run when I need to clear my head. Lately, I have been running because of Nash's drama he brings.

Maverick is first to walk through the front door. I give us both water before I start upstairs to get a shower. I hear a knock at my door and run back down the stairs.

"Hey Jake, I just got back from a run with Maverick. I need to shower, then I will be right back. Make yourself at home."

I make it back downstairs, and Jake is playing with Maverick. A few moments pass. It's completely silent. I look at Jake, wondering why he hasn't said anything.

"Jake, why are you here?"

"I don't want to be the one to tell you Kallie, but I need to."

I look at Jake, worried. "Nash was late for your graduation because he was out with someone else."

"Excuse me, what?" I said sharply.

"I am so sorry. You're a good person and any man would be lucky to find someone half the woman you are."

I just sit down and start crying. Jake pulls me in for a hug.

"It must be so hard for you to hear this. I didn't want you to find out from someone else."

I just nod. My eyes start to fill up with tears.

"Kallie, do you need anything?"

"No, I just want to be alone."

I run upstairs. I climb into my bed. I feel like my heart is breaking. How could he do this when he means so much to me? I knew he was jealous of Holden. I can't believe he would cheat on me because of my friendship with Holden. It seems so ridiculous. I should text Holden to tell him he was right; Nash was only going to break my heart. I cannot forgive Nash. He has gone too far this time.

I hear Maverick running up the steps as Jake opens the door. Maverick enters first, Jake follows. He comes to sit on my bed.

"Kallie, I don't want to leave you alone. I know what it is like to have a broken heart. You need a friend."

Jake is right. I roll over to face him. I nod. Still unable to speak.

I grab Jake's hand, "Stay." I whispered.

He sits in my chair across from my bed.

I can feel him watching me. My eyes are red and puffy. I scan his face as he is searching for words to say. At this point, nothing he says will make me feel better. I don't even know why I asked him to stay.

"Nash never deserved you, Kallie."

I am too upset to even think straight. I almost fall asleep until I hear a knock on the door. Jake quickly gets up. He tries to quietly walk down the stairs. The knocking is more forceful. I listen as he opens the door.

"She doesn't want to see you," Jake said.

"Why are you here, Jake?" Nash's voice is sharp.

"Kallie knows you were cheating on her; I knew she needed a friend, so I came over to check on her."

"Tell Kallie to answer her phone." Nash snaps.

"Leave her alone for the night."

Jake sounded annoyed. Nash sounds angry. He has no right to be angry Jake is here. He literally just broke my heart.

Jake makes his way back upstairs. "I made you lavender tea."

I gently sit up in bed. "Thank you, Jake." I whisper.

"Nash was here. I told him you didn't want to see him, but he insisted you answer your phone.

"I don't want to speak to him." I barely manage to say.

I look at the chair Jake is sitting in. "How do you know about him cheating?"

He shifts in the chair. "It was the photo on Instagram."

"Do you know how long they have been together?"

"No, I don't."

"Do you know who she is?"

"Yeah, remember the son I told you about?"

I nod. I still can't form a sentence. I wipe the tears falling from my face.

"That is her." Jake whispered back.

I can tell Jake is holding back some information. I roll over to face the wall.

"Kallie, I never wanted to hurt you."

"I know."

The morning sun is really starting to shine through my windows. I really should get a black-out curtain for them. I grab my phone off the floor. I open my Instagram. First thing I see is a post from Nash at a concert with her. I feel my heart breaking again. I feel angry. It confirms everything I have been wondering all night.

I lay in bed for what seems like hours. Maverick is barking wanting to go outside. I let him out. Nash still isn't home. I need to stop thinking about where he could be. He could be at work or with Willow.

I should just pretend I have no idea Nash is cheating on me. He hasn't confirmed it or denied it. Jake did tell him I know. I grab my phone. I open Nash text I decided to send him a text. Me: Where are you? We need to talk soon.

Nash: Yes, we do. Can I come over tonight?

Me: Yes. I will be home.

I go take a long shower. I sit down, crying as the water washes over me. No matter what today brings. I need to be strong. Jake has warned me Nash is cheating on me. The worst part is hearing it. Now I need to see if Nash will confirm it. The worst part, I still live next door. I get out of the shower; Nash is sitting on my bed.

"Hey."

"Hi." I lied. I can't keep strong.

"You want to go out tonight?"

"No, Nash. I want to know who that girl was in your insta post? Is that why you are distant and made up some excuse to not come to my graduation?" My voice is cracking as I try to yell at him.

"Kallie, I didn't want you to find out this way, but yes. I thought if I pushed you away, you would move on. I saw Jake's car at your house."

"Jake was here. I needed someone. It was like the night of my graduation you disappeared. Holden came to celebrate with me. Jake was here last night. They both were here celebrating last week. You seem to never be around when I need someone."

Nash paces. I can see the guilt on his face.

"I never deserved you, Kallie."

He looks me in the eyes. He is holding back the tears. They are full of regret. He doesn't speak a word to after that.

"I was offered a promotion at work Nash. I wanted to celebrate. Since you made it clear you don't want to be a part of my life, I didn't include you."

He still hasn't said a word. I feel like I am dying inside.

"Just leave Nash."

I refuse to cry in front of Nash, he doesn't deserve to see me cry. He slams the door on his way out. The anger starts to creep up. I am so hurt and angry, I don't even want to see Nash right now.

I call for Maverick, "Let's go for a run, I need to clear my head."

I am grateful this town has three major roads. I make it to third street. I stop at Coffee and Book. I order a white chocolate mocha and Maverick a Water. I half smile at Willow. I want to believe she has no idea what is going on. I find a table outside. I pour Maverick's water in his bowl. Willow comes to sit with me.

"I don't know what happened between you and my brother, it's not my business. He showed up at my apartment drunk going on about how he messed up."

"He did. And I can't forgive him this time, Willow."

"Do you love him, Kallie?" I take a pause, "Yes, but he keeps hurting me emotionally. I don't know how much more I can take."

"You're my friend. I don't want to see you upset; you do need to figure it out."

Maverick looks exhausted. "I am going to take Maverick home." We slowly walk back to my house. I walk through the doorway. I feel more alone than I should.

It's my home, clouded by memories of Nash. Some good and some bad. Our first fight happened right here in the doorway. It seems so stupid now. I look around my house. I can't help but to think about everything going on. The rage trickles through my body.

How can I hate him when he means so much to me? I can't even convince myself to leave him alone. I know I need to. It also puts a perspective on my friendship with Jake. I don't understand how Jake can be so open and honest with me when the one person I love the most can't.

I decided to call Jake. I want a friend here to take my mind off Nash. Judgment clouds my thoughts today. I greet Jake at the door. I wrap my arms around his body. I give him a small kiss on his cheek.

"Thank you for being a good friend to me." I whisper in Jake's ear.

He wraps me in his arms a little tighter. "You have no idea how much of a good person you are, Kallie."

I walk with him to my kitchen; I watch him sit on my counter.

"I know you don't want to hear this, but I think it is better for you to leave him alone completely." I watch Jake place his arms on his hips.

"I know, it's just I don't understand how I gave someone my all and he gave me nothing in return."

"He gave you a headache."

I let out a small laugh as I nod. Nash sure did give me a headache. He also made me realize I am not the villain. I will never settle for less again. I look up at Jake as he sips his coffee.

"We should invite Willow over and have a movie night in."

"I think that is a good idea. However, I am pretty hurt and angry about the situation."

I watch him text Willow. "Every heart break needs a good laugh and cry. Tonight, we will do both."

I should have known texting Jake to come over was a bad idea. I suddenly just want to be left alone. I keep pushing through this conversation. I am so distracted by my emotions and my thoughts. I barely hear what Jake is saying. I pour myself a cup of coffee.

Jake jumps off my counter; I watch him start walking to my couch. Maverick is sleeping on my couch. Jake startles him.

"I can bring Marlee over so Maverick can play with her."

I agree, mostly because I like seeing Marlee. I get ready for tonight. I clean my house and take a shower. When I am alone in my thoughts, I get angrier with Nash. While my heart is breaking, he is totally fine, it isn't fair at all. In this moment, I decided I am going to make him regret cheating on me.

I set on snacks on my coffee table with Willow. She brought coffee cakes, and I am so happy about that. We wait for Jake to arrive with Marlee before we decide on a movie for tonight.

"My brother really is stupid sometimes."

"I would agree."

"I would ask how you are doing, but I think I know."

I smile back at her just as Jake walks. We watch the dogs start running to the back door. I let him outside with the door cracked so they can come and go as they want.

"They are so cute together." Willow said. She starts to me smile. "You know you two would be cute together."

I look at Jake and we both laugh.

I sit between Jake and Willow. Willow picks the movie. I hate any movie where a dog dies, and she picks the one type of movie that would make me cry. I pull my knees to my chest; I realize I cannot hold back the tears burning my eyes.

"I told you this is what you needed." Jake said.

"Yeah, yeah. I do feel better." I said.

"Nash is an idiot, you deserve better." Willow said.

Willow leaves after the movie, since she has to be at work so early tomorrow. I walk her out when I notice Nash's truck is at his house. I really hope he doesn't come over while Jake is here. I don't want to deal with his attitude, but at the same, I don't owe him anything.

Jake stays around to help me clean up after our movie time. We destroyed the snacks that Willow brought. Moments like this make me realize how grateful I am to have friends like them. I wish Holden was able to come tonight.

I wait for Jake to leave. However, I know Nash would be insane if he decided to come over here. I make sure to lock all my doors before going to bed. I don't want him to even try to come near me. I am trying so hard to convince myself I am fine. I know eventually I will be fine. It just hurts.

Maverick follows me to my room. I turn on my tv to help me fall asleep. I already hear Maverick in the corner snoring. I will never understand how he can fall asleep so fast. I feel like it takes me forever.

14

Nash

I don't like seeing Jake at Kallie's house. I don't like seeing Holden at Kallie's house. I don't like how I am feeling. I am out of control. I need to feel pain from something. I am ready to beat the hell out of Jake for even telling Kallie about me cheating on her. It wasn't his place.

I pace more, waiting to see Jake leave her house. I know he has to go to work today. I wait until I see him outside of her house.

"Hey Jake, wait!" I yell out to him.

I rush over to him.

"What?"

Before I can say anything else, my first is slamming into his face. Blood running down his nose into his mouth. I watch as he tries to step backwards.

"What the fuck, man?"

"You did this."

"No, I am not the one that hurt her, I am just the one that wouldn't stand by while you were doing your usual shit."

I see him take another step back. Fuck, I hear Kallie opening the door and Maverick running over to us.

"What the hell Nash!!"

My eyes lock on her.

"Go home now."

I watch her guide Jake back inside her house. Probably to clean the blood off his face. The look of disappointment on her face stings harder. I know I shouldn't take my anger out on him or her. I can't help but to be so angry that he is the one that told her. I have to find a way to make it up to her.

I turn on my heals making my way back to my house. I slump into my couch; I pull out my phone, looking for flowers to be sent to her. I think she has work today. I know Holden will not be helping me with this mess. I can imagine Willow is just as angry with me since the last time she was over here we go into it. I wish I would have told her about Emma and how complicated it is with her. I just want my son in my life. Surely everyone can understand that. If not, I need Kallie to understand the need to have my son with me.

I finally find flowers to be sent to Kallie's work. 24 roses. She has to forgive me after seeing the arrangement. I wrote a note, but I know she probably will not read the damn thing. I enter my debit card information and now I need a nap before I go to work. I used to love night shift and now with everything going on, I hate it.

I sleep on the couch, hoping the sound of her car will wake me up. It didn't. My alarm woke me up. I look out the window. Kallie is alone. I force the courage to go over there. I slide on my shoes; I want to make sure Jake or Holden aren't coming over.

I slide on my shoes and make my way over to her. I knock on her door. She opens the door and her face drops.

"Nash, no."

"I didn't even say anything."

"Because I am speaking first. I got the flowers. It doesn't excuse what you did. I need time to think and process. You literally cheated on me."

"I know."

I stare into her ice-cold eyes. I never knew her eyes could be cold. I really did push her to her limits on this one.

"I will give you space."

I turn to walk away. I hear her shut the door once I am out of her driveway.

I don't know how she can avoid when I live next door to her. I hope she finds a way to forgive me. I know hurt her; I also am not stupid to think it will be quick, but for my own sanity, I hope it is quick.

I don't work today. I just want to grab a beer and start drinking. I resist the urge. She would be so proud of me. I broke her and, in the end, I broke myself. I will not stop proving that I am worth of her and her love but first I need to fix my relationship with Emma. I need to find a way to have my son.

I grab the mustang keys and head to Emma's apartment. I am lucky she lives in the city. I rub my clay hand down my jeans and after I pull into a parking spot next to her car. I walk to her door.

"What do you want?"

"I want to see my son."

"I told you he isn't your son."

"My patience is running thin. You can't use that kid against me. I will take you to court so I am able to see him."

"Good luck. Your reputation has reached far and wide. I am surprised your girlfriend is still with you."

"Emma, don't. We both know what happened. We both know if there was any truth to the story, I would be in jail. And since I'm still here, you know damn well it is a lie."

She slams the door in my face. That could have gone better. I run my finger through my hair. I turn to walk away; I can feel her stare on the back of my head, probably wishing I would leave this alone. If that is my son, I want to be in his life.

I get into the mustang. I start hitting the steering wheel out of frustration.

"Fuck!"

I still don't feel better about the situation. I start driving to relieve some stress and anger that is building up. Without even thinking, I pull into Coffee and Books.

"You look rough."

"Well, Willow, I just came from Emma's."

I see her eyes go wide, searching for words.

"I take it you and Kallie still aren't speaking?"

"No."

Willow hands me a large coffee. "You deserve this."

I wish I had work because I am going crazy. I wait for her to ask more about Emma. I already know she thinks this entire plan is insane. Hanging out with her again so I can get her to trust me. Also while keeping Kallie close to me.

15

Kallie

It has been a couple of days since I've spoken to Nash. Usually me running to my car. It is so awkward. I really try to avoid him. I never make eye contact with Nash anymore.

I need to talk to Nash. I can't keep avoiding him. I can, but I hate running to my car. I take Maverick outside. I see Nash is in his garage. Now is the perfect time to speak to him. I muster the courage. I pace in my kitchen, trying to figure out what I want to stay. It is now or never. I have the courage.

I walk quietly to Nash's garage. Of course, he would be in it working on the Mustang. I stand in the doorway until he notices me.

"Hi, come in."

I nod and walk fully in. I can feel the tension in the room.

"Is the mustang ready for racing?" I cross my arms. I feel so uneasy.

Nash glances up, "Yeah, almost."

It is really awkward now. I huff. I watch Nash stand up. He walks slowly towards me. I tense up. He must have noticed, since he stuck his arm out for me. I glance between his hand and his eyes. I take his hand and he pulls me close to him.

"Kallie, I need to tell you how I feel about you. I am still in love with you."

I have waited too long to hear these words. I just stare back.

"I never should have cheated on you; it was a lapse in judgment. I fully apologize and regret it."

I'm searching for words to say back. "Nash, it isn't OK. It isn't fair to me. All you do is hurt me." He comes u behind me. He wraps his arms around my waist.

"I love you Kallie, you are the only one I want." I sigh. I want to believe him, but I can't.

"Kallie, I'll never be able to make it up to you, but I promise, I can treat you right."

He starts caressing my arms. All the progress I have made it's gone. I crave this man. I take a sharp breath, "lets go inside." He guides me to his living room. The skylights are letting the moonlight shine brightly. I can almost see the stars. The way the moonlight is reflecting off his eyes, I can almost see the sincerity in them.

"Nash, all you manage to do it hurt me. I don't know if I can believe you." I'm fighting back tears. I want to believe him, time and time again. I keep getting hurt. I take a deep breath. "I saw the photo of you and her at the concert, that is what was so important you could barely see me."

"I saw Holden's car at your house."

"Nash, you can't tell me who I can be friends with!" I am yelling, trying to hold back the tears.

He pulls me to his chest; "I know. I just don't want to lose you. It terrifies me."

Nash holds me as I fall apart in his arms. "Hey babe, it's going to be ok" he gently kisses my forehead. I need to tell you about my promotion.

"My internship turned into a full-time job. I was asked if I could move to South Carolina to work in editing. I couldn't say no." I watch as Nash processes what I just said.

"Kallie you can't leave. We still have so much left in our relationship."

"Nash you just cheated on me. I can't keep getting hurt by you."

He pulls me into his chest, tilting my head back up to meet his eyes. I pull him down to my level. I take his mouth in mine. I feel his tongue getting more aggressive. I push further into his body. I pull him back with me. I swipe my arm to clean of the counter behind me. Our mouths are still locked together. He picks me up and places me on top of the counter. He swiftly takes off my pants and I am grabbing his shirt over his head.

"Are you sure?"

"Yes."

I can't control myself as he glides his hands up my thighs. I wrap my hands around his neck and my legs around his body. His hands are tangled in my hair. I can feel him sliding in and out. My legs start to shake, letting him know I'm close to going over the edge.

"Just breathe baby."

I let out my lungs.

"Moan my name."

"Nash."

I sit there trying to control my breathing, realizing what just happened. I jump off the counter and quickly grab my pants to slide them back on.

"Nash, I never should have came here tonight. We really can't keep doing this. I refuse to be treated this way."

"I promise, I can treat you better. You have to give me a chance."

"No, I am all out of giving chances." Nash is pacing. "Nash, I literally can't do this anymore. It is draining me."

Normally, I would call Holden. He is busy tonight. I need a distraction. I start to pace around my kitchen. My eyes keep going to Nash's house. I call Jake. He asks if I want to come over to get away from Nash. I tell him yes. I grab Maverick and go over. He meets me at his front door. His arms are wide open. I rush into them.

"I am glad to have you as a friend."

"No matter how things end with Nash, I will always be here for you."

Jake has always been so good to me. He is a great friend. I sit with Jake while Maverick and Marlee run around the living room. I watch him try to find something to watch on T.V.

"Do you want to play a game?" He asked.

"Yes."

He goes to the closets and pulls out a risk. This game can literally take hours, which would be a great distraction. Jake probably knows I need it. I am actually really good at this game. I feel my phone vibrating in my pocket. I am hesitant to pull it out in case it is Nash.

Willow: Where are you? Nash called me.

Me: Of course he did. I'm with Jake playing risk.

Willow: I will see you tomorrow. Have fun. ;)

I laugh at the wink face she sent. Even she thinks I should leave Nash alone for good. I know this is what I need, but I almost feel like he needs me more than I need him. I look up, when I noticed Jake was smiling.

"It is good to see you smile again." Jake said.

"I know. It has been a while, actually."

It is my turn. I watch Jake slowly walk to the kitchen to make us coffee. That's the best thing about Jake. I never have to tell him what I want. He seems to always know. Willow's words keep repeating in my mind. "You two would be a cute couple." Isn't it too soon to start dating Jake? Maybe I am reading too much into it. Jake brings back two cups of coffee.

"Cream, no sugar, just how you like it."

I smile at him. "Thank you."

The game is almost over. Jake looks like he is getting tired. I should leave with Maverick. I get up to leave. Maverick and Jake follows me to the door. I give Jake a hug good bye. He leans down to kiss me. I wrap my arms tighter around his neck. I start to pull away.

"I am sorry, Kallie. I shouldn't have crossed that line."

"No, don't apologize. I will see you later?"

He nods.

Maverick is barking while sitting next to my car. While I am driving home, I start to think about the kiss. I still can't believe Jake kissed me. How did I even get into this situation? I have to call Willow.

"Jake, kissed me as I was leaving his house."

"Oh? I better get all the details!" Willow said.

"Come over, we will have a girls' night."

I hang up with her. I was pulling into my driveway when I noticed her car was already in my driveway.

"I was at my brother's." Willow said as I got out of my car.

I laugh. "Well, that must be awkward."

We go inside. I make us a glass of wine while we talk about Jake.

"I can't believe he actually did it."

I look at her, confused.

"I knew he liked you and had feelings, but never imagined he would actually act on them."

"Yeah, Jake is so reserved. I never expected he would try anything."

"Forget Nash, Jake is better for you, anyway."

I take a moment to reflect on it. "You're right. After everything Nash has put me through, I deserve to be happy and do what I want for once."

It is getting late. Willow has had too much wine, so I set up the guest bedroom for her. These past few months, the guest room has actually been used. My mind keeps going and going. I decide after I set up Willow for the night to go to my office.

I love my office. I have an electric fireplace and it is so cozy in here. I place my coffee on my desk and begin writing. I start writing about all my emotions, everything that has happened with Nash and I. Everything.

Suddenly Maverick starts barking. I must have fallen asleep while still typing my story. It is morning. I go downstairs to see what is going on. Willow is giving Maverick breakfast.

"I let Maverick out and gave him breakfast. I am about to leave, but I will see you tonight?"

"Yes, I didn't forget."

I walk her out before laying down on my couch. I feel like I didn't even sleep last night.

16

Nash

I told Kallie everything. I thought I would feel relieved, but I didn't. I know she is falling apart right now. I can still see her face when I close my eyes. I didn't mean to say she doesn't deserve me. I meant I didn't deserve her.

I called Willow to come over. I hear her opening the front door. I turn around from my couch.

"I told Kallie how I felt."

"And?"

"Well, since you're here and not her, it's safe to say it didn't go well."

"Why are men so stupid?"

"Why are girls complicated?"

"Bro, you literally cheated on her, snuck into her house, and beat the hell out of Jake." Her eyes glance down. "It's a lot to process."

"Has she said anything to you?"

"Not about you. And no, I will not tell you because she is my friend, too."

"Kallie is leaving for South Carolina."

By the way she is looking at me, I feel like she already knew this. I exhale sharply. I grab a cigarette from my jeans.

"You knew?"

"Yes. We all know. Jake, Holden and I."

Of course, they would all know before me. I have to convince her to stay here, to make it right with me.

"Hey Willow, do you think you can tell me anything else I don't know?"

"No. We are going out this weekend, so leave her alone. I will try to talk to her."

How can I even convince her to stay when she won't even come near me? And when I do see her, she looks away quickly. We had sex on accident the last time we did talk. I shouldn't have pushed her that far. The way she kept looking at me. Her eyes drawing me closer.

My sister has even taken her side. I can't blame her at all. I wouldn't want my sister to date someone like me.

"I keep seeing Jake's truck at her house."

"Are you spying on her?" Willow crosses her arms. I know at this moment I have fucked up.

"Well, no, I was just looking out my window."

"I don't believe that at all."

We sit in silence. I almost forgot she was here until she asked for water. Maybe Willow is right and I need to move past this and give her space. But now that I know she is leaving soon with Holden, it makes me worried, angry and hurt. I can't be without her, it's already killing me not being able to talk to her.

17

Kallie

I am supposed to go hang out With Willow today. It makes my heart happy that we are still friend even though Nash, and I ended things pretty roughly. Maverick's barking alerts me she is here. I rush down the stairs.

"You ready to go out?" Willow said cheerfully.

"Yes, I need to go get out."

I get into her car. "Where are we going?"

"A party." I give her a look.

"You're in college. You're supposed to go to parties."

I smile, "I just graduated, remember?"

"I have friends that invited me and I am inviting you." Willow said.

I am nervous; I have never been to one ever. I feel like I haven't really experienced college. I try my best to smile. I can't stop thinking about what Jake would say. I push those thoughts out of my head. I just want to have fun tonight.

Willow parks her car. We have to walk a little. I don't mind since I am wearing flats. Once we arrive, two guys hand us a drink. I am skeptical, so I just hold it. I watch Willow down hers.

I walk up the stairs to go inside the house. The music is so loud, way too many people for my comfort. I let out a deep breath. I didn't realize I was holding. Over to my right are a few people playing beer pong. I walk past them, trying to see if I knew anyone.

"Kallie. Kallie." I turn around. I kind of recognize him.

"I was in your classes."

"Oh, hey. Did you graduate?"

"No, I actually am two credits short."

"That's cool."

I find myself starting at him awkwardly.

"I am going to go find a drink." I stated.

I scan the house to find the kitchen. I decide to play it safe and grab a beer. I figured one should be fine. I listen to the music and watching beer pong. This is exactly what I imagined a frat party to be like.

It feels like an eternity of me sitting here. I check the time, only three hours have to pass. I have to find Willow. In the next room next to me, she is dancing on the makeshift dance floor. At least she is having a good time.

I am not having a good time. "Willow, let's go."

"No, Kallie."

I roll my eyes. "I will drive home."

She continues to argue with me. "Fine Willow."

I help her down the stairs. She can barely walk. I know she can't drive. I grab the keys from her as I place her in the passenger seat. I text Jake. I am dropping Willow off and I will text him when I get home.

I start driving home. I hate driving in the dark. It gets hard to see on the two lane roads. I also have a fear of deer jumping in front of my car. I get off the interstate, it is only 15 minutes to Willow's house now.

I noticed a car coming into my lane. I grab my phone. I tried to swerve. I lose control over the car. It starts flipping. Over and over again. It finally hits a tree before stopping.

Willow's car is upside down. I search for my phone. It's hard to move. My face is covered in blood, my body is hurting. I reach up to press the SOS button.

I wake up in the hospital. Jake and Nash are by my bed. Jake looks relieved and worried. Nash looks a mess. His eyes are puffy.

"I am so happy you are awake." Jake said.

He stands by my bed, he gently takes my hand in his. Nash goes to get the nurse.

"Kallie, do you remember anything?" Jake's voice is low.

"A little. I remember a car coming at me head on and it flipping."

"Anything else?"

"No."

His eyes start to tear up when the nurse comes in.

The nurses check over me. "The doctor will be in soon."

Nash comes to my bedside. "Do you know what day it is?"

"Saturday." He sighs, tears falling from his eyes.

"Guys, tell me what is going on now."

The doctor enters the room. Nash and Jake look at him.

"Well Kallie, you were in a terrible wreck. We had to put you in a medical coma for two weeks. You had swelling on your brain and we had to fix your face."

I feel like my world is crashing down on me.

"What do you mean, fix my face?"

"We had to construct your nose and eye socket. Your face has a few lacerations from the glass, cutting it. We also had to remove glass from your face."

I don't speak. I can't speak. The doctor leaves the room.

My eyes start to tear up. "Where is Willow?"

The boys look at me and at each other. A few moments pass. Nash wipes the tears from his eyes. "She didn't make it."

"We thought we lost you too Kallie." Jake is trying to hold back his tears.

"What happen that night?" I asked.

"A drunk driver was coming at you head on. You swerved and lost control of Willow's car. You were able to push the SOS button before you blacked out." Jake wasn't able to continue.

"When Willow arrived at the hospital, she was intoxicated. She didn't have her seat belt on and was ejected from the car." Nash's voice fell flat.

"I am so sorry Nash. I only had one drink. I wasn't even tipsy by the time we left. I never meant for Willow to get hurt."

"I know. They took your blood count too. It was only .001."

I place my hand over my face. I can't help but to thing this is my fault. I can never forgive myself. Willow died because of me. Nash tries to pull my hand off my face.

"Kallie, this isn't your fault." I still can't speak.

"Kallie, look at me." I hear Jake walking towards me. He sits on the bed next to me, placing his hand on my knee.

"We are so happy you are alive right now. Please don't blame yourself."

I look up. "She wanted to drive. I couldn't let her drive. I took the keys and placed her in the passenger side. I forgot to buckle her seat belt."

I can tell Nash wants to change the subject. "Do you want to see your face?" After hearing the news about Willow, I forgot my face was messed up. Jake helps me to the mirror.

I don't even recognize the person staring back at me. I have a scar from the top of my face down my nose to my lip. I have smaller cuts on my cheek and it's all red. I can't believe this is my new face. I hate how I look now. I can't help but to wonder if Nash or Jake will find me pretty anymore. I can't even find myself pretty anymore.

"Has anyone called Holden?"

"Yes, he comes by every day after work. He told us to call him as soon as you woke up." "What about my job?"

"Holden said he would take care of that.

Jake calls Holden for me. He said he would come by after work. I can't wait to see him. I keep falling asleep due to the medications. I wake up to Holden standing by my bed.

"You had me so worried you weren't going to make it, either."

Tears are streaming down my face. "Willow didn't make it."

He looks down at his feet. "I know Jake told me. I've come to visit you every day since Nash called me."

"Nash called you? Not Jake?"

"Nash wanted to be the one to tell me. They both were a mess, but Nash was able to speak more words than Jake."

***

It's been a few days since I woke up. I get released today. I know Maverick will be happy to see me. I am sure he has been having fun with Marlee and Jake. I still feel weak when I walk. My right leg isn't as stable as it should be. Nash and Jake offered to help me as much as possible. I am so grateful for that.

I can tell something is going on with Nash. He offered to stay with me while I recover. Honestly shocks me because of how things ended with us. I never expected him to offer to help me. Especially since I killed his sister. My heart breaks for him.

I walk through my front door. It's clean. Jake and Maverick are patiently waiting for me. I selfishly just wanted to be alone tonight. I force a smile for them. Maverick comes running to my side. I gently pet the top of his head. He sits at my side and huff. "I know, but I am still so sore, Maverick."

I still need more time to process everything that has happened. They were able to grieve Willow; in a week my whole life was turned upside down. I lost my friend. My face is scared. I don't know if I even still have a job; Holden says I do. I still can't shake the feeling I will not be able to go to South Carolina.

Jake brings down my blankets and pillows from my bedroom. "Do you need anything else?" "My phone charger and water, please."

I text Holden. I am home and Jake is here tonight, so he doesn't need to check on me. Jake returns to my living room. I thought it would be easier for you to sleep on the couch. I brought your book down here as well. I glance over at the coffee table.

"Did you clean the place while I was gone?"

He shakes his head. "Nash heard Maverick barking. He came to check on him. Nash knew you were out with Willow. He called me looking for you. When I told him I hadn't heard from you, that's when he went to Willow's house. He saw her car and the cops. He brought Maverick to me and told me what happened. He wanted to believe you were going to be fine. He cleaned your whole house, and we took care of Maverick."

I nod my head. "Thank you for taking Maverick."

"Kallie, I can confidently say we both would do anything for you."

I can feel my eyes start to water. Jake moves closer to me. "I can leave for tonight."

"I thought I wanted to be alone. I really need you to stay."

He wraps his arms around me. I am so glad at that moment I have a friend like Jake. He doesn't ask for anything in return, but always lets me know I am important to him.

"Jake, does my face look terrible?"

"Kallie, it looks different but you are still beautiful. You have the most beautiful soul I have ever met. Your looks are just a bonus."

I shake my head.

"My looks were everything to me."

He pulls away from me. "Kallie, you are so much more than that."

My tears are flowing even harder now. It is hard to breathe. I know I shouldn't care about the small things. I should be happy I am even alive. Here I am worried about my unfamiliar face.

Jake lays a blanket over me. "Do you want me to stay down here or go upstairs?"

"Down here is fine." I suddenly realized with his height the oversize chair wouldn't be comfortable. He doesn't seem to mind.

I don't think I slept much last night. Between the alarms for my medication and the guilt of Willow, sleep just seemed impossible.

I am still so sore. Jake has to go to work today. I am going to miss having him here with me. Nash is supposed to come by today. I think it is going to be awkward. I can't help but to wonder why he doesn't hate me. I am finally left alone with my thoughts. Maverick jumps on the couch by my feet. He places his head on my hip. I start thinking about what if Willow drove us home vs me driving home? I start thinking about how we shouldn't have gone to that party. My mind is racing with what if scenarios. My heart breaks for Nash and Willow's friends. It suddenly comes to me, Coffee and Books was Willow's dream. What will happen to the coffee shop? Would it be too much for Nash to handle to keep Willow's legacy going?

Nash slowly enters my house. He looks so heart broken. I wait for him to speak about Willow, before I ask about anything.

"Do you hate me, Nash?"

He looks confused. "No, I lost my sister and thought I was going to lose you. I don't hate you."

He looks down at his feet. "I am scared I am going to lose you too soon."

The raw emotion across his face lets me know he wants to talk. "It's ok to talk about it with me." I said.

"I don't know what to say. I have a lot on my mind with the funeral, the coffee shop, her apartment. It all falls back on me."

I pull on my lips. "It will all be ok. You have to believe it's going to be ok. Even when your world is falling apart."

"I don't really believe in hope." Nash's voice falls flat.

"Hope is all we really have in life Nash, nothing is ever guaranteed."

"I know. My sister was only 21."

A few minutes pass. I still can't find the words Nash needs to hear. "It's almost time for your medications."

I nod my head. "Are you taking my to my physical therapy today or should I call Holden?" Nash nods his head. "Yeah, I can go with you."

I still can't shake the guilt I feel when I am around Nash. It is suffocating. I can't take this feeling anymore. I need to push my feeling aside and let him help me. He is just trying to show he is grateful I am still here. I need to start realizing my life isn't as bad as it could be right now.

"Nash, I still need help to get dressed."

"Ok, what do you want to wear? I will go grab them and help you."

"A t-shirt and shorts, can you grab my converses? I think Jake put them back in my closet."

He returns with my favorite shirt and my shorts. He helps me get dressed. "I never thought I would be doing this while we were young."

"What do you mean, Nash?"

"I always thought I would help you get dressed when we were old and could barely stand."

I smile. "I can barely stand now."

"What are you going to do with Coffee and Books?"

"I am going to continue Willow's legacy. I need help, so I was going to hire a new manager."

"Willow would want people to continue to have access to good cheap coffee and good books."

"I know. I have to be honest with you Kallie. I own it. I bought it for Willow. I knew it was her dream, and she was struggling with money."

"You really are a good brother."

I wish the circumstances were different. I see changes in Nash that are beneficial to him. He seems like he needs a hug and told it is going to be okay. In the grand scheme of life, my face isn't as bad as it could be. It makes me unique now.

We arrive at my appointment. I am nervous, I've never been to physical therapy. I am worried my leg will never be back at 100 percent. At this point, I just wish the pain would stop. He grabs my arm. I take his hand. "I am sorry. My leg just hurts so bad."

"It's fine. I want to help you."

After my appointment, he takes me home. He helps me back to my couch. His eyes start to water. "Are you ok?" I asked

"No, I am trying to be so strong, but I feel so weak. I don't know how I can ever recover from this." He sits down on the floor next to me.

I pet his head. "It is ok to cry. It doesn't mean you are weak."

He starts crying harder. I try my best to hug his neck. He reaches up for my arm and grabs it. It is silent for a while. Maverick comes to lie by Nash, putting his head in his lap.

Holden silently enters the room. My eyes meet him as he observes Nash mid break down. Holden sits by Nash. "I am here now. If you want to leave."

Nash doesn't say anything. He walks out. Holden asks about Nash and how physical therapy is going. He pulls out an envelope from his pocket. It's from our boss. I sigh and open the letter. He says to take all the time I need and hopes I am better soon.

"He doesn't expect you to be back so soon. He knows how bad the wreck was and you were."

"Thank you."

"What do you want for dinner? I know you haven't been eating."

I forget how well Holden can cook. I want to take a shower, but I can't ask Holden to help me. That would be weird. I wish I could walk better. I could make it up the stairs. I will wait for Nash to come back.

18

Nash

I feel like I am dying. Willow was only 21. She had her whole life ahead of her. And Kallie. Kallie is lucky to be alive. I should have been there. I could have saved Willow. I could have driven and prevented this whole thing.

I haven't slept much since the accident. It felt like my heart stopped when I saw Willow's car laid on the roof. I knew it was going badly. I never expected my heart to be ripped from my body.

Kallie is finally awake. I am happy and relieved. However, my heart still aches for Willow. I try to push my feelings down that Kallie did have a part in killing my sister. My heart is ripping apart. Scratch that, my heart isn't whole to begin with.

I am battling with how can I even look at Kallie without feeling a bit of betrayal in me? I sit at the hospital with her, Jake and Holden. I see how Jake looks at her, trying to comfort her. Tell her everything is going to be ok. I almost feel he is saying it for the both of us.

When Holden comes, I can tell by his glances towards me, he regrets what happens too. I can tell he feels like I do and wishes he was there. I am glad she has someone like Holden in her life. He doesn't owe Jake or I anything and they here he is making sure we are good at staying with her at all times.

Even when it's hard to look at her, he places a hand on my shoulder and tells me, "she is alive."

Willow is — was — my best friend and sister. I agreed to help look after Kallie once they released her from the hospital. Since I live next door, it will be easier for me. I want Kallie to come home. I also need time to process everything. I know she regrets what happens, but at the same time, her words feel empty. It is wrong of me to feel this way since she was the one that tried to prevent from being hit by the drunk diver.

I hope this grief doesn't last long or I will break.

19

Kallie

Between Jake, Nash and Holden, I am never alone long enough. Jake tries to encourage me to try things on my own. Holden gives me updates at work and life. Nash wants to take off me and help. When all three are here, I feel like I am going crazy.

I asked Nash to come over. I need a shower. He is the only one I feel comfortable enough to help me with that. It is still awkward because he sees me naked and almost helpless. I hate how only Jake seems to care. I know Holden cares, but I feel like a burden to him. I feel like Nash is only here to see the guilt I feel. I refuse to be my own worst enemy. I am determined to take a shower on my own. I have to start proving that I can do things on my own.

I am once again alone with my thoughts. I accidentally killed his sister. I can never forgive myself. Nash will never forgive me. I am the constant reminder of that night. The scars on my face and body will always bear the guilt. I look down at my semper fi tattoo on my wrist. I can't help but to think about how much I care about Nash. My tears fall harder in the shower. I am reminded of how much I love this man. The water falls over me, washing away the tears for him and Willow. I will always feel so guilty about that night.

I wobble my way to the kitchen. I pour a glass of whiskey. I slide down my cabinet until I am reaching the floor. Maverick comes running to lie beside me. I bury my face in his neck. I can feel the hot tears running down my face. I am crying so hard I am gasping for air. My ears are pounding. Maverick places his paw gently on my arm. I look up at him. Nash is standing in front of me. I quickly wipe the tears from my eyes.

"I didn't hear you come in."

Nash sits beside me. He pets Maverick. He wraps one arm around me.

I hear him sigh, "I don't blame you Kallie. It was an accident. You didn't cause the wreck."

I feel my eyes start to water. "It never would of happen if we didn't go out."

He wraps his arm around me. "You don't know that."

He helps me up. "Lets get you in a hot bath. It might make you feel better." I watch him throw dried lavender into my bath. He helps me step in. "If you want, I can see if Jake can come over."

"No, I just need to get my feelings out. Evey time I look at you I see the pain I caused you. I have the guilt of her death with me. You had time to grieve, I didn't."

"We all thought you weren't going to make it. I couldn't bare to lose you and my sister at the same time. The doctor told all three of us to prepare for the worst." I bury my face into my hands.

"I can't even close my eyes any more without seeing the pain on your face anymore. My face is the reminder for you."

It's silent. I can't take it. "Nash if you don't want to be here you don't have to be."

"Damn it Kallie, Why can't you accept the love I am trying to give you?"

I suck in my bottom lip. "I don't deserve it."

"You don't deserve it?"

He looks at my face. I see his eyes turning red. "I think I will call Jake when you get out."

I nod my head. "I think I need more time."

My heart felt like I ripped it into a million pieces. I sink lower into the water. I don't try to hide the tears streaming down my face. My head and ears are pounding.

"Jake is on his way. Do you want to get out?" I barely manage to say yes. It was more of a whisper. He helps me get dressed.

"Call if you need me. I promise I will be here." I nod. I can't speak. I lay in my bed waiting for Jake to come up.

I hear Jake knock on my wall. "Did you want your drink you made?"

I don't speak.

"I can't even begin to understand how you feel right now. I want you to know Holden, and I care about you, Kallie. We don't want anything to happen to you." Jake hands me my drink.

My voice is weak. "Can you promise me one thing, Jake?"

"Yeah, what is it?"

"Promise to never lie to me." My voice is shaking.

"I can keep that promise."

I hear my phone vibrating. I ignore it. "Its Holden." I nod. He answers my phone. I hear him tell Holden I don't feel like talking. He walks to the corner of my room. I hear him tell Holden he is worried about me. I am worried about myself too. I have this guilt for killing a friend. I destroyed Nash. That is a lot of guilt to carry. I wish I could hear what Holden was saying. I finish my drink quickly. I pull the blankets over my head so I can cry in peace.

"Hey Kallie, do you want me in here or the other bedroom?" I don't respond.

I feel Jake climbing onto my bed. "Kallie, you cannot hide forever. I promised I wouldn't lie to you, and I promise I will never leave you alone." I try my best to roll over. "Take all the time you need, but you have to realize this isn't your fault. A drunk driver hit you head on. You are lucky to even be alive."

I pull the blanket back. "Willow isn't so lucky. She died because I wanted to go home. I should have let her sober up there." Jake rubs my head until I calm down.

I hate myself. I can't sleep. I can't stop playing back the words Nash said to me. How can he even be here when everything is my fault? Physically, I feel strong with physical therapy. Mentally, I feel weaker around Nash.

I wake up to the sunshine of my face. I search my bed for my phone. I feel Jake next to me. "I am so sorry Kallie, I guess I fell asleep trying to sooth you."

"It is fine." I pause. "I do appreciate you helping me."

"Is Nash coming today?" Jake asked.

I look down, "No, we think it is best if he took a break from me."

"Do you mind if I come back after work?"

"If you want, I should be fine. I really do feel stronger with the physical therapy."

I am not sure if he believes me. I know Jake notices my limp. My leg does hurt, but it is bearable. I don't mind having Jake around. He does seem to make me feel better about the situation. I know I have to be okay on my own.

I stumble down the stairs to let Maverick outside. It is raining today. I step outside to feel the rain on my face. I close my eyes and look up at the sky.

"Kallie, I really don't want to leave you alone." His voice is low.

"I have to do this. I am barely alone anymore to be able to try on my own."

He nods his head and gives me a hug.

I watch Jake leave. Now it really is just Maverick and I. I look over to Nash's house. He is outside as well. I try to hide from him, if he wanted to see me, he would come over. I have to give him space and I want nothing more except to take him in my arms. I call Maverick to come back in. I start to make coffee when I hear the back door open.

"Kallie, can we talk?" His voice is low and serious.

I slowly nod my head. "Yeah."

He envelopes me in his arms. "I am so sorry Kallie." He drops to his knees. I wrap my arms around his neck, caressing his hair.

"Nash, I am the one that should be sorry. It was my fault." My voice is breaking as I hold back the tears.

"No, you needed me the most, and I left."

I feel him crying. I can't find the right words to say. I just hold Nash as he breaks down. I try to help him up because my leg is hurting. "Come to the couch with me."

"Kallie, I promise I will never leave you again. I love you so much."

The tears just start streaming down my face. "I've heard this before and you never keep your promise."

"I realize now I was too close to losing you and the pain I felt. I never want to feel again."

I can't find the words I need to say. "How can you forgive me, Nash?"

"It truly was an accident. You didn't do it intentionally. You couldn't have known going out would have caused any of this."

He takes my hand. "Can I make you coffee or tea?"

"I was making coffee before you came in."

Nash confuses me. I don't understand how he is fine being around me now when, a few days ago, he couldn't even look at me. My heart is breaking for him. I have to stop with the self pity. This isn't about me, this is about Nash. I have to set him free of me. I can't keep doing this. The back and forth, the broken promises, the never ending fights.

Nash checks the time. "I have to go to work, but I will be back later." "I will be fine tonight."

After Nash leaves, I call Holden. It is almost 4th of July. I need to get out of town. We usually go to the lake on the holiday. We make a plan. I need to ask Jake if he will watch Maverick. I decided to call him.

"Hey Kallie."

"Hey, are you busy this weekend?"

"No, why?"

"Can you watch Maverick while I go out of town this weekend?"

"Yeah, bring him by. And are you sure you will be fine to go?"

"Yes, my leg just has a limp right now, I am getting stronger every day."

I make Jake promise not to tell Nash I am planning to leave for the weekend. I don't want him to know or try to stop me. The new scenery will be good for me and my mental health. I hate how he keeps treating me like I am disabled. I hate this internal battle within myself. I feel like I am slowly losing my mind.

I really need to get away to get my focus back. I just feel so broken and beat down. I know it someways this is my fault. I didn't buckle her seatbelt and I knew she was too drunk. The guilt will always be with me. I have to learn to accept it. I also know, I will never be beautiful again. I have lost my confidence, I have lost my beauty, I feel like I am nothing.

I go to take a shower by myself. I turn the water hot. I sit on the shower floor, letting the water fall over me. I start to cry, with the water falling on me it washes them away. I want nothing more than to be in Nash's arm with him telling me it's going to be okay. I start to convince myself pushing Nash away for good this time is what I need. We both need it.

The water is turning cold. I decided to get out and put on my comfort pj's with puppies on them and an oversize t-shirt. I climb into bed, I can't stop thinking. I start writing notes to do for tomorrow. I need to pack and clean my house. I hate leaving when my house isn't clean.

I wake up to the sun rays hitting my face. I absolutely love the way the warm sun feels early I the morning except for today. I get out of bed to start doing everything I need to. I let Maverick out and make my coffee. I go outside to sit with him, when I look over I see Nash staring back at me. I look away quickly and so does he. I feel my heart breaking all over again. I call for maverick, we go back inside. I grab a cup out of my cabinets for my morning coffee.

I will quickly clean and pack. I don't want Nash to see me leaving with Maverick. I don't feel like answering questions. I slip on my favorite ripped shorts and a band t-shirt. I love this shirt but it is technically Nash's. I slip on my sandals since we will be at the lake. My body is killing me today.

I tell Maverick to go get in the car. I really should have called Holden to help me. I struggle my way to put my bag in my car. I have good days and bad days with my leg. Today is a bad day. I start to drives to Jake's house. I drive past the wreck scene. I am so grateful I don't remember much from that night. I feel my eyes begin to water. I fight the urge to cry. I don't want Jake to see me cry today, I feel like that is all I ever do anymore. I remember all the times with Willow. The good, the bad, and the in between. Somehow, Nash always creeps into those memories.

I miss watching movies and eating her twist on popcorn. It always had to have candy in it. The late night chats while at the coffee shop. I push those out of my mind as I pull into Jakes drive way. I check my eyes and sit in my car for a minute. I have to see Jake. I have to go to the lake with Holden.

20

Nash

Seeing Kallie so helpless and hopeless is killing me. I knew I would need time and I also feel like she knows I was here because I love her. If I didn't love her, I sure wouldn't be here.

I wish she would see how badly I was breaking on the inside. I look at her and keep seeing her and Willow. Kallie got a second chance, and all she is doing is feeling sorry for herself. It's dumb.

Her pity party is driving me crazy. She needs to move on. I took my own advice and while I am healing from losing my sister; it has also been months. I see her growing stronger every day. I know she doesn't need Jake, Holden, or me over here every day, but here we are. She doesn't seem to process that we care about her, that we want to be here because we love her. We stronger I push her, the more resistance she gives me.

I take Maverick outside. I let him run for a while. I go upstairs expecting to still see her in bed. To my surprises she is in the shower. I knock on the door before entering.

"Yes?"

"It's me. Can I come in?"

"Sure."

I glance down at her body in the shower. She still has some nasty scars over her body.

"Do you need anything?"

"A towel."

I hand her one from the closet. She turns off the water, standing there dripping wet while waiting for me to pass her a towel. My dick is growing uncomfortably hard while looking at her.

She steps out of the shower. Her nipples are so hard. She motions for me to come closer.

"Take me to my bed."

I pick her up and carry her to bed. She pulls me down with her.

"Are you sure?"

She nods and I move to take off my shirt. She wraps her arms around my neck and pulls me closer. I look into her blue eyes, her auburn hair still soaked. I start rubbing my hands down her body, stopping at her most sensitive spots.

"I need you Nash."

I take my jeans off. I hear her take a deep inhale. I touch her center. She is already dripping wet.

"I need you in me," she says as she pulls me closer to her.

I inset inside her, waiting for her body to respond. I slide in and out of her, trying not to hurt her. She wraps one leg around my back. Forcing me to go faster and harder. I feel her body beginning to shake. I can't hold it. We let out a groan together.

"Do you want me to help you clean up?"

"Please."

I help her clean up and I slide back into bed with her. I wait for her to say she regrets that. She wraps my arm around her. I slide my fingers down her spine. I grace over her scar on her back.

"How are you doing?"

"I'm doing better."

"Nash, I am sorry for how I have treated you."

I tilt my head unsure of what to say. We both have been through something traumatic. I don't want to make this about me so I settle on saying nothing.

Thats the thing about us. I know how she feels about me and she knows too. Before the accident we weren't speaking. Now I don't want to waste anytime we have together. Time goes too fast. If I have realized anything about losing Willow is that time is precious, and it goes too fast.

21

Kallie

"Hey Jake, thanks for watching Maverick."

"It's no problem. Marlee will be happy to see him."

I give Jake all of Maverick's things while letting Maverick jump out of my car.

"Don't forget, I will be home on Sunday morning. I was planning on stopping by to get him before I went home."

"yeah that is fine."

He gives me a hug. "Be safe, Kallie."

"I always am."

I really need to get away from this town. Everywhere I go, I am reminded of Nash and the memories of him. It's almost time to pick up Holden.

I watch Holden put his bags in the car. I set my navigation system to the condo his dad owns. It's only five hours from the lake. I am beyond ready to leave.

"Have you spoken to Nash?" Holden asks.

"No, I've seen him outside. He's never home anymore. It's it pretty easy to avoid him." I can feel the pathetic sounds in my voice.

"We are going to have a fun weekend. You will not even think of Nash." Holden is full of surprises to keep me busy this weekend.

I watch Holden look out the car window. "What's on your mind, Holden?"

"I am just enjoying the view. Usually I drive. It is nice to take in the scenery." He is oddly quiet on the trip down.

"I see you and Jake are getting closer."

I laugh. "He is a friend. He was there for me when I found out Nash was cheating and after the accident. I hear Holden breathe deeply.

"I don't want to see you hurt again. It was brutal."

I nod my head.

When we get there, I want to go to the lake.

"I want to go on the boat, or even find a bar nearby."

"Ok, we can do that. Do you want to go swim too or just a boat ride?"

"I don't care."

"The gps says we are five minutes out. Is your dad's condo on the golf course?"

"No Kallie, it's right on the lake with his own private dock."

I knew his dad had money, but I had no idea he was a rich kid. I am relieved to see I don't have to walk far to reach the condo's door. I look around inside. I can tell it is just a summer place for them. They only decorated it with lake photos and golf awards.

"I will make you the best Moscow mule ever!" Holden seems too excited to make a drink after that car trip.

"Fine, I am always down for a drink."

My phone vibrates. Hey. Where are you? I ignore it as I listen to Holden talk.

"Are you looking forward to moving?"

"Yes, but I am nervous. South Carolina is a vast change. I always knew I wanted to live closer to the beach again. I didn't think it would be this soon. Physical therapy is going well, so there shouldn't be any issues with that."

Holden pauses. "I leave after we get back from vacation."

I need to get away from Nash. He will never heal with me around. I just want a guilt free weekend and forget all the pain. The pain I hate to admit is making me feel like my world is crashing down. Now, I find out my best friend is leaving once we get back from the lake.

I watch the waves from the boat while sitting on the back deck.

"This is a view I wouldn't mind seeing every day."

"Soon you will, Holden."

He glances at me. "Do you need another drink? You look like you do." He grabs my mug before I could say anything.

Of course, I do. I want to get drunk enough I forget about everything about Nash. "Thank you. I needed this."

"Let's go swimming." I put on my swimsuit. Holden just shakes his head. It's not a long walk down to the water. He dives in from the dock.

"Come in. The water is great."

I take a deep breath and dive in after him.

"Liar, this water is chilly."

He swims up behind me, "Then you clearly have not had enough to drink." I watch as he climbs on into the boat. "My dad always keeps a little in the boat. You never know when you may need it."

"Your dad is a smart man." I take the bottle. Holden and I keep passing it back and forth. He puts the bottle back on the boat.

Holden picks me up and throws me into the water. He quickly realizes we need food. I want a shower. The lake makes me feel gross.

I get into the shower first. This water feels amazing. Holden is right. I do need food. I feel so drunk. I get out of the shower. Holden is already making grilled cheese for us. I sit at the bar. "Thank you. I am starving." He sits next to me on the other bar stool.

"Are you ready for the weekend to really get started?" Holden asked.

"Yes, this is the best weekend I've had in a while."

Later that night, we find ourselves at the bar. We walked here so my short legs were tired. I grab a drink from the bartender. I follow Holden to the pool table.

"Do you know how to play?"

I look at the table. "A little and I am terrible."

He half smiles, "I love to win, so it will be a great game."

"I told you, I am terrible at this game."

"Kallie, you didn't even get one ball into the pocket."

I laugh. "Ok, so horrible." I watch Holden take a sip of his drink. I walk over to the ring toss.

"I am going to play ring toss." Holden looks at me.

"It's a game with a circle thing on the string. You try to get it on the hook." He nods, trying to process what I am talking about.

"It is harder than it sounds." I am up first. I got it on the hook 3 times out of 10.

"Your turn Holden." I watch Holden. He gets it 5/10 times.

"How is this your first time? You are so good at this game."

"I am naturally talented."

"It is almost closing time. We should start walking home."

I finish my drink. "Ok, let's go."

We start the short walk home. My legs feel like Jell-O and painful. I just need to sit down for a moment. I know we are close to the condo. Holden looks at me with concern.

"Holden, my leg really hurts.."

"You are stumbling everywhere."

I grab a hold of Holden's arm. He helps me finish walking to the condo. "Almost upstairs, Kallie"

Holden wake me up, "We are going for a boat ride. I cannot wait to show you the river." "Holden, It is so early. GO away!"

"No, get up it is 11:30." I angrily throw off my blanket.

"Good, now get dressed."

I put on my swimsuit. I find my long sleeve fishing shirt and shorts to go over.

I meet Holden in the kitchen, he made me a glass of orange juice. I pick it up and nod. I am finally awake enough. I slide on my shoes.

"I am ready now."

Holden grabs the keys off the bar. We walk down to the dock. I get into the boat. It is a beautiful boat. I watch Holden climb into the boat. He starts it and pulls out of the dock.

We start to go down the river. This is a pretty big place. "Holden, we need to come back here for a longer time." "Yeah, we should try. There is a lot of fun stuff to do." "I am hungry." Holden pulls up to a dock. It is a seafood place. We get our food to go. We start back for the condo. "We need to pack and clean up the condo." I nod. "Okay lets head back.

I am not ready to go home. I am ready to pick up Maverick from Jake. I know Marlee and Maverick are having fun playing. I trust Jake has taken great care of Maverick. I hope Maverick isn't being too wild for Jake.

"I will drive home." Holden and I pack my car. "I really wish this weekend wasn't over so soon." I smile at Holden. "Me too. It went by way too quickly." I turn on the radio. I really hate all the commercials. I switch to my music app. I find my favorite playlist and hit play. "Your taste of music is so vast. You never know what will play next." "I like to keep you guessing." "Have you thought anymore about South Carolina?" I pause before answering. "Yes, I have. I am going to see if I can leave sooner. The new job is a once in a lifetime thing." "Do you want to be roommates? We would be able to get an apartment on the beach if we are." "I wouldn't mind being room mates and living on the beach." "That does sound so perfect. No more shoveling snow or salting the driveway. My only worry is hurricanes coming." Holden is giggling. "It isn't that bad. It's just different."

I drop Holden off at his apartment. I drive to get Maverick from Jake. I have to tell Jake I made my choice. I pull into Jake's driveway. I hear Maverick and Marlee barking. I get out of my car. "Hey Jake! How was Maverick?"

"Maverick was great. They played a lot in the backyard. Maverick slept on the couch."

"Sounds like a great time." I follow Jake inside. "So I decided to take the job in South Carolina." He smiles guiltily. "Really. I am so happy for you Kallie." "Thank you. I wanted you to be the first to know. "I am glad you did." "I couldn't tell you, Jake. You are part of my life. I should get maverick home."

Jake looks so sad that I decided to go. I pull into my driveway. Nash is outside. I am so anxious. I take a deep breath. I open my door and watch as Maverick jumps out of my Mustang. He runs straight to Nash. "Maverick come." He looks at me and slowly trots to me. "Sorry about Maverick." Shakily tell Nash. Nash glances at me. "It is ok. Where was he while you were gone?" "He went to spend the weekend with Jake and Marlee." Nash looks down at his feet. "He could have stayed with me." I gently smile back. "I didn't want to impose. Oh, and congratulations on the engagement." "You heard about that?" "It is a small town. They offered me a job in South Carolina. I decided to take it." "Oh, when do you leave?" "In about 6 weeks." "I will miss you." I am unsure of what to say now. "I really do need to get Maverick inside."

Maverick and I walk back to our house. I open the front door and he runs straight to the couch. "You're such a lazy dog, Mavi." That went fairly well, telling Nash I am leaving so soon. I lay on my couch. I have six weeks to pack my house. I should start. I am so sleepy from the drive back home. I think I will take a nap.

22

Nash

I noticed Kallie's car hadn't been home all weekend. I wonder if she is with Jake or Holden. Did Maverick go with her? I know I shouldn't care. I feel a deep regret for how things ended with Kallie. I just want to know where she is. I will text her.

I almost feel guilty. I am supposed to falling for Emma. I can't. I may never forgive her. I am scared to even touch her.

I text her and she doesn't respond. She has to be with someone she cares about. I hate feeling like this. I go
see Emma. I am proposing today. I really do not want to. I want Kallie in my life, but I also want my son in my life. I have already missed three years of it.

After that night with Kallie, I have noticed she moves away from my touch. She won't answer my calls or text. It's like something flipped, and she hates me again. I know she will hate me once she finds out what I am doing.

I hear Emma coming from upstairs. If she only knew how much I wanted her to be Kallie. I run my hands through my hair while I pour her a cup of coffee. I smile as I hand it to her. Her green eyes are staring back at me almost seems like they are empty.

"Something on your mind?"

"Are you done taking care of Kallie?"

"She left, and I don't know where she went." I give her a shrug.

I see her eyeing my phone. I pick it up and slide it into my front pocket. I don't need Kallie to text me and start a fight with Emma. Not when I am this close. We both know one call from Kallie saying she needs me. I would drop everything to be there for her. I lean against the counter next to Emma, waiting for her to say anything.

"You need to tell her to leave you alone."

"She hasn't texted me at all."

I see Kallie's mustang pull into her driveway. I hope Emma doesn't notice this. I lean in closer to her. I feel her place her lips on my neck. If she only knew I was just trying to get a better look at Kallie and Maverick. I wrap my hands around Emma's back, pulling her closer to me. My phone starts buzzing in my pocket. Emma pushes away from me.

Kallie: Wow, couldn't even wait until I texted you back.

Me: it's not like that. I promise.

It stings lying to her, but I want to tell her in person what is going on.

Fuck, why can't I be normal?

I wait for Emma go get ready and go to work before I can talk to Emma.

Emma goes to get ready for work and I try my best to make it seem like I don't want her to go, but honestly, I can't wait for her to leave. I keep my eyes locked on the window, looking out to Kallie's house. I feel so guilty about what I have to do now.

I give Emma a kiss on her forehead before she leaves. I wait for her to pass the stop sign and turn before walking over to Kallie's house.

I knock on her door. She opens with door with Maverick.

"That is Emma. I am just doing this so I can see my son without her flipping out."

"Did you get the DNA test?"

"Yes, it came back as mine."

She lets out an exhale.

"Nash. I can't keep doing this. We aren't good for each other and I realized that while I was on vacation."

"Let me guess, with Holden?"

"Yeah, every summer we go to the lake."

Kallie's face scrunches as she looks over my shoulder.

Fuck, Emma is back.

"What the fuck Nash!"

"I just came to see if she needed anything."

"Ya know, good luck with that," Kallie laughs out.

I see the rage on Kallie's face. I step in front of Emma before she can hurt Kallie.

"Don't worry, I was just leaving," Kallie says.

Where she just got back.

I grab Emma by the wrist and lead her far away from Kallie. I don't need her going crazy and actually harming Kallie. I might lose my shit and say forget the whole deal if she ever harmed her in any way.

We get to my porch and Emma slaps me.

I deserved that.

"I told you to not speak to her."

"Emma lets get one thing straight now. You are not my mom or sister, you cannot tell me what I can and can't do."

"Do you want to see your son?"

"Obviously."

"Then you will do as I say."

Damn this bitch.

I look over to see that Kallie watched the total scene happen. There goes what little pride I had left. Sometimes, I wish I could hit Emma and knock some sense into her. I would never actually hit her. Hitting women is against my morals.

Emma readjusts herself closer to me. I feel her arms wrapping around me from behind. I roll my eyes and pull her hands off of me. Just seconds ago, she was yelling and slapping at me. Now she acts like everything is ok.

She follows me inside, my eyes follow her movement.

"What is wrong with you?"

"Emma, don't start."

Her lips fall in a straight line. I can tell she is searching for the words.

"You know, I am the best thing that ever happened to you."

Lies. Kallie was.

"Mhm. And Carter."

"I should go get Carter and bring him here."

I get he wanted to go to camp. I am just glad it's not a stay away camp. Emma finally leaves to get Carter. Maverick's barking alerts my attention. I should go talk to her. I see her outside with Maverick throwing the ball. I walk out of my garage, deciding between if I want to talk to her or not, I sit on my stools, propping my face against my hands.

"I saw Emma leave," Kallie said, as Maverick runs to me.

"She went to get Carter."

Kallie nods in agreement. "Are you happy?"

"I guess. I know it shouldn't be this way. I shouldn't have to pick between my son and someone I love."

"Nash, stop. It shouldn't be so hard to be with someone, either."

I shrug. I don't know what to say when she has so much truth behind her words.

Kallie recalls Maverick. She pauses and looks back before she leaves. I can tell she is struggling to leave. If Emma saw her here, she would lose it. Let alone if Carter saw Kallie and me together. That would be terrible.

The garage is a mess. Tools and car parts are everywhere. I turn on music and start cleaning up the garage. I open the toolbox to place all my tools in there. I place a wrench inside. The memory of Kallie giving me it comes rushing back. She was so proud and excited. It really is the most thoughtful gift I received.

I hear Carter laughing and yelling for me.

"I am in the garage," I shout back as I walk out.

"Look what I made at camp," he says while pulling out a decorated pinecone.

"It's for the birds."

"A bird feeder. Let's fine a place to hang it on the trees."

Carter grabs my hand, pulling me to the porch.

"Can I hang it here?"

I look at the nail in front of the window.

"Yeah buddy."

I hang the pinecone up while Carter is jumping up and down excitedly.

"Now I can watch the birds."

His little smile makes this situation worth it. Well, almost. Carter, being happy and safe is all I care about.

"I'm going to show mommy."

Carter runs inside to find Emma. I see she is standing by the bookshelf. I rush inside.

"Looking for a book?"

"No, I was just looking at the photo of you and Willow."

My eyes cut down to my feet.

"I miss her."

"I'm sure you do."

I need coffee.

"I need to go check on Coffee and Books."

I hired a few people to keep the place running. It still does not require any of my time. That I am thankful for.

I walk in and notice right way how busy it is. I walk into the office.

"How is everything going?"

"It's going well. We have increased sales and figured out ordering."

"Do you need anything from me?"

"No."

I nod. The office is still the way Willow left it. A few photos of us from the opening hanging on the walls.

"Would you like to take these photos?"

"No, they can stay here for now. If you ever need anything, call."

I was hesitant to hire just anyone to be the manager. Lauren was highly recommended. Just graduated, looking for a job desperately. She seems to know what she is doing. I let her hire 2 more people as baristas. It seems to be working and maybe the reason for sale increase. Now that more people know about this place. Willow wanted to keep it a small-town feel, which was fine, but wasn't a lot of business.

I order a coffee, prolonging the need to go home.

"What's the name for the order?"

"Nash."

"What can I make for you?"

"Black coffee."

"2.75."

I hand him my money. "I've never had to pay for my coffee before."

"We don't hand out for free."

"Good to know," I say with a chuckle.

This kid has no idea who I am. I see Lauren coming out of her office while my coffee is being made.

"Here is your drink, Nash."

I smile.

"Lauren, I will see you next week unless you need anything before."

The barista gives Lauren a look, scrunching his face. I turn to walk away when I hear her say, "That's the owner."

I am half tempted to look back to see the horror in his face. Instead, I keep walking. I need to go home.

Emma is making dinner. I know I shouldn't complain, but I really miss cooking what I want. I am so tired of chicken.

"Mommy made chicken nuggets."

"I knew I smelled something good."

I give Emma a kiss on her cheek as I wrap my arms around her. She presses her body harder into mine. Her hair is up, leaving me access to her neck. Slowly, I brush my lips across her neck. I glance over my shoulder. The tv entertains Carter. I whisper in her ear, "Maybe tonight we can open the bottle of wine."

Emma lets out a little laugh. "Carter is exhausted. Maybe we can take a shower, too."

I release her so she can finish cooking. I set the table before joining Carter in the living room. I sit on the couch while Carter is on the floor.

"Do you want to get on the couch?"

"No, I like being down here."

I slide my phone out of my pocket. No notifications. While I am not surprised, I am a little disappointed nothing from Kallie. I know she said she wanted space, but I didn't think she meant it this time.

23

Kallie

I get back home and I still can't stop feeling guilty about leaving Nash like that. I walk to my backyard. I see him standing in his kitchen. I look away fast. All I wanted was fresh air. I take a moment before I walk back inside. Something inside me is telling me to go over there. My actions say otherwise.

I feel Maverick brush up against my leg. I pet his head and decide to go over there.

"Why did you leave without telling me?"

"I—I thought if I left, it would be easier on you. I leave for South Carolina soon, anyway."

"Kallie, I told you a million times. I don't want to leave you alone."

"Damn it. Why — why can't you just let me go? You don't need the constant reminder of what I did."

He grabs my hand. "No."

"No, what?"

"I am not letting you run from your problems."

"You can't tell me what to do. I want to do this, I am and will. You can't stop me."

I hear him breathing louder. He rolls his eyes. "Come with me Kallie."

He takes me by my hand. "Your knee still bothering you?"

"No" I lied.

"We need to have a talk about us and our future."

"Nash, I don't want a future with you." I suck in my lips to bite my bottom lip. "I can't have a future with you."

I see the heartbreak on his face again. This is exactly why I didn't want to come here. I knew deep down it would start something because we don't know how to just be friends. He will always try to make sure I am fine and want more than I can give. I can't even give myself grace and time. Why would he ever expect me to have anything more?

"I need to go." I rush as fast as I can down the stairs back to my house. I check the time. I text Holden about Nash. Holden: he shouldn't expect anything from you right now. And you are being way too hard on yourself. Me: yeah, I am just trying to cope with everything. But I will be back at work tomorrow. Holden: Can't wait to have you back.

I throw my phone on my couch. I should prepare for work tomorrow but of course, that is a tomorrow problem. My laptop is charged and my bag is packed.

I feel like it is time for me to go back to work. I am stronger and better. I also do not want my promotion to be taken from me. Jake enters, breaking me from my thoughts. It is an ice surprise to see Jake.

"I brought Chinese food. I got you noodle."

I smile at him. "Thank you."

"I really need cheering up. I had a rough visit with Nash. I told him I didn't want anything from him and he needs to let me go."

"I mean, you have to do what is best for yourself."

"I know, and I am going back to work tomorrow."

"I am so proud of you Kallie."

I look at Jake, confused. "Why?"

"It's the first real step to get back to normal you have taken."

I nod my head. Jake is right. It is the first time I've tried to get back to normal. I pick up my noodles. I didn't realize how hungry I was. The next step is taking care of myself without having everyone dropping in.

"Do you think people like me deserve to be happy, Jake?"

I observe the puzzled look on his face. "Yes, yes, you deserve to be happy. You are such a good person, you made one mistake."

I move closer to him, placing my head on his shoulder. He wraps his arm around my shoulder blades. "It is getting late. I should shower and get ready for work tomorrow."

"Can I help you?"

"I think I got it, but you can stay if you want."

I watch him pace around the living room. "Are you alright, Jake?"

"Yeah, I just know how Nash is, and I don't want any trouble."

"I think with the circumstances, it will be different this time."

"I don't know Kallie, the man is in love with you."

I have to push all emotions aside. "Its getting late, I am going to bed."

I head up the stairs, with Jake following me. I have noticed he likes to stay here after Nash and I fight. I never asked why or put Jake in an uncomfortable situation, so I just let him stay. I climb into bed. My mind starts racing. I am nervous about going to work tomorrow. My first day back since the accident. I toss and turn all night.

I feel like I just fell asleep when my alarm starts going off. I get dressed before going to make coffee. I start to make my way to the kitchen when Jake startles me. I let out a gasp.

"Hey, sorry, I didn't mean to scare you."

"It's fine. I didn't sleep well. I was coming to make coffee."

"It's already made."

I will miss when Jake doesn't come over anymore. I like having someone else to make my coffee. I pour some coffee with a splash of creamer in my favorite travel mug. Jake tells me good luck and I grab my keys to leave for work. Luckily, there is no traffic and I don't have much time to get lost in my thoughts. I park next to Holden's car. I guess he forgot I was coming today, so I walk up alone.

I go past the office ladies straight to our office. "Kallie, I would have waited for you, but I forgot you were coming today."

"It's fine, really."

I observe the half dead flowers on my desk, and fresh flowers.

"Who sent these?"

"The dead ones are from the front office and the fresh ones were delivered this morning before you got here."

I sit in my chair to read the note left. Dear Kallie, I am sorry for being an asshole. I miss you and want to see you soon. With all my love, Nash. I hold the note in my hand read it over and over again.

"Kallie, you ok?"

"Yeah, it is just from Nash. We had a massive fight."

He can tell I don't want to talk about it, so he drops it. I open my laptop to check emails and start working. I want nothing more than to just curl under my desk to break down. This shouldn't be so hard. He should get the message by now. I truly do not understand how to push him away for good. Maybe this is just us. The fighting, the distance, the makeup. I feel like I am just surviving. I want to live.

I push all those thoughts out of my mind. Finally, I have a manuscript of my interest. This will keep me busy for the rest of my day. I decided to work through lunch. Partly because I don't want to be left alone with my thoughts and partly because I have a lot on my to do list this week.

I check the time. "Holden, when are you leaving?"

"I am actually about to leave. Do you want to get dinner?"

"I would, but I really want to go home."

He gives me that look. "I promise, I am fine." I think I sound convincing.

We walk to our cars. "If you decide you need someone tonight, call me. I will come over as soon as I can."

I give him a hug. "Thank you for being here for me."

"Always."

Now it's finally time to be alone. No Holden, Jake or Nash coming over. I know Maverick misses seeing Marlee, but I just want to hang out with my dog. I snuggle up on the couch with him. Maverick places his head on my chest. "I know Maverick. Soon we will be leaving here and hopefully my leg will heal quickly." I pet his head.

I must have fallen asleep. I woke up to my phone ringing. I answer Holden's phone call. "Check your email." I check it and see all the new updates for work. I am glad to be back, it keeps my mind distracted, I don't miss the strict deadlines. I have a two more manuscripts to read this week. I need to catch up quickly. I have a lot of spare time now so it will not be hard.

I get back to work since I need to focus. I love my job and help people make their dream a reality. I glance at my phone. It is 2 am. I see I have a missed call from Jake. It is too late to call back, so I will wait until tomorrow. I head up the steps to actually go to sleep before I have work tomorrow.

I wake up and get dressed before making my morning coffee. My leg only hurts a little today, so that is progress. I still limp. My doctor is hopeful that I will be back to normal soon. I make a mental note to schedule my physical therapy. I shimmy into my pants. I slowly walk down my stairs. I really hope my new apartment doesn't have so many or my leg is fixed by then.

I check my phone and see a text from Jake. I just wanted to check on you. I haven't seen you in a few days. I smile at my phone. At least I know someone actually cares. Come over tonight.

I am finally ready for work. I let Maverick outside. I watch Nash pace in his kitchen. He looks concerned or scared. Its hard to guess which one. I am still doing my best to avoid him. I call for Maverick to come back inside. I pet his head before I slide on my shoes.

I go to work and really focus on what I am reading so I can edit. Maybe I wasn't ready to come back. I thought I was but the more I try to focus, I can't stop thinking. The day is really dragging. I push it out of my mind. I place Nash's flowers on the floor by my desk. It was really make me think of him, and think of these last few months.

I leave work, I cannot wait to get into my pajamas and curl on the couch with Maverick. I stumble my way to the kitchen to make lavender tea. I hear my front door open, I am not expecting anyone here tonight. Jake slowly walks to my kitchen.

"You forgot I was coming tonight?"

"No, I just had a long day at work." I only half lied.

"I can leave if you like."

I ignore Jake's statement as I pour him a glass of lavender tea. I look back at Nash's kitchen window. He must have walked off once he saw Jake here. My suspicion is only heighten at this thought. Nash will never leave me alone. I don't know how to be more clearer to Nash.

I see the way Jake is looking at me. I promise him I am fine. I am not going to mention the flowers or Nash being Nash. At least Jake is supportive of me leaving for South Carolina and isn't trying to change my mind. I have never been more sure of anything in my life. I belong in South Carolina, and deserve my dream job. I have worked so hard to get here. What I do know, I like spending time with Jake.

24

Nash

I know I shouldn't care, but it's always Jake or Holden. Why can't she have any other friends?

Right because willow died.

Ugh. I wipe my hands down my jeans. Stressed and needing a cigarette, I go to the garage. Maybe I can get some peace while I am down here. I haven't been racing and now that summer is almost over, there are 3 races left. The mustang must be feeling neglected.

I hope Jake is everything I wasn't for Kallie. I have to focus on Emma, but at this point I wouldn't be angry if she left, told the whole world I hit her. It would be a relief to get away from her and make things so much easier.

I text Jake. I want him to know that I approve of him and Kallie. Even if I really don't, they have spent a lot of time together since she got back. I have my own situations I have to deal with.

I grab a beer before I sit on the bar stool. I close my eyes, remember the time Kallie was in the garage after a bullshit fight and how I pulled her close to me. I could feel tears escaping from her eyes. Tears of joy and sadness all mixed together. How every fight about Holden seems so mundane after everything we have gone through together. I wish she didn't feel the need to push me away. And yet here I am sitting alone in my garage wondering how everything became so fucked.

Oh right. Me.

Life is funny that way.

Equal parts pain, misery and happiness and love.

I wish Willow was able to see how much I loved her.

A knock on the side brings me from my thoughts.

"How ya doing?"

"As good I as can," I say, pointing to the beer.

"Ya know, Willow would be proud of you. Still managing Coffee and Books along with working a job you love."

"Jake."

He glares back at me.

"Your sister would be proud. She is probably looking down at you're right now, laughing at how you are drinking beer while figuring out how to keep going."

"Probably."

I raise my bottle to him and he raise it back.

"To willow."

The silence is loud. The voices in my head are louder.

"I just wanted to check on you. You haven't had much time yourself."

I nod in agreement.

"One last thing, have you lost your damn mind having Emma back into your life?"

I smirk, "Well, yes and no. I have a plan and I think it is also failing, like everything else in my life."

"Nah, you just have to stop feeling sorry for yourself. Man up and get your shit together."

Ouch.

He's right. I need to stop and actually work on getting my life back on track. I was doing so good until I saw Kallie and had to have her. It is a struggle. I know I am not good for her, but I also know I don't want to live without her.

"I won't hurt her, ya know."

"Yeah, which is why your face is still together."

His eyes lock on mine.

"But make no mistake, if you fuck this up, I will hunt you down."

"Calm down, I don't plan on fucking that up.

I hand him another beer. I miss hanging with him doing nothing. The peace that Jake brings is relaxing. I feel at ease, like everything is simple. Jake is my longest friend, probably the only one that understands me the most. To be honest, I don't think Kallie understands me the way Jake does.

"I should probably go before the storm comes," he says as he slides his phone back into his pocket.

"Kallie?"

"Do you really want me to answer that?"

"Well, no, I don't."

He leaves and goes next door to her house.

Emma and Carter went back to their house, so here I was, all alone. I don't mind being alone, but when I have a distraction next door, it's hard to focus on anything. My bedroom isn't safe since it faces hers. I let out a huff.

I decide to make dinner. Pizza and beer are the perfect combination. I make a microwaveable pizza and try to find something to watch.

Why is it so hard to find a movie? Kallie only likes horror movies, so it was easy to find one that was interesting or terrible to make fun of it. I settle on a movie I've seen hundreds of times with Willow.

I pull out my phone to text Emma. It is late, so she is probably sleeping. I wait for a response. I place my phone next to me in case she does respond. The movie was over and still no response from Emma.

I go to my room, a shower sounds nice. I get undressed in my room. Kallie's light turning on catches my attention. I turn to face the window when I see them kissing and her pushing Jake on the bed.

I slowly walk to my shower. I look up at the stars, admiring the view from my shower. I finish my beer before hopping in the shower. It looks like a storm is coming. I hear the rain starting the drop on the roof. I take a quick shower. Storms can get intense quickly in Iowa. My phone is making a horrible sound. Tornado Warning. Crazy how quickly it can intensify here. I look at the notification. I should go see what the news is saying.

I leave my bathroom and notice Jake and Kallie are no longer in her room. I rush down the steps to turn on the tv. The weather is reporting damages a few towns over.

"Wanna come over since the storm is getting bad?"

I stare at my phone.

"Yeah, be right over."

I rush through the rain and wind.

"It is windy already," I say as I walk through the door.

"I know how you are in storms. I didn't want you to not take it seriously," Kallie said.

I sit next to Jake while we watch the metrologies talk about the storms. Kallie pulls up storm chasers on her phone that are in the area.

"It has already caused a lot of damages and leveled some neighborhood."

The poem starts flickering as the sirens are going off.

"We should probably go to the basement now."

Jake and I follow behind Kallie. She grabs our flashlight.

"I have lanterns and snacks in the basement."

Jake sits on the couch. Kallie is searching for lanterns while Jake is finding the weather. The power starts to go out. I hear Kallie's breathing increasing.

I text Emma if they are safe. I get a response. "Carter is freaking out."

"You can't leave. The storm is here."

I straighten my face. "I know. I am just worried about Carter."

We wait out the storm in silence. Jake holds Kallie a little tighter as she watches the tornado rip through the city, making its way to us. I keep checking my phone for updates from Emma.

The sirens are blaring, it sounds like a train outside.

"It's here," Jake says, while grabbing a blanket. I text Emma, waiting for any update. I start to panic when I still haven't heard anything.

"The towers are probably down."

The tornado passes. We go to assess for damages. Our houses are fine. A few trees are down.

"I need to go check Coffee and Books and Emma."

I leave for Coffee and Books. Luckily, Lauren pulled all the outside tables inside for the night. I check the doors and windows. They seem fine. I'll come back once it's light outside. It is a way too hard to see with a flashlight.

I head straight for Emma's apartment. I drive there in half the time. Some roads are closed. I finally make it to her. Carter looks terrified.

"How is your apartment?"

"Damages. The windows are broken."

"Grab some things and come back with me. My house is fine."

I pick up Carter. At least he has shoes on with his pajamas.

"Are you ok?"

"That was scary."

"Lets go wait for mommy in my truck."

Emma throws some stuff in the backseat with Carter.

"Did you get my blanket?"

"Yes."

The car ride back was silent. We take in the damages of the trees, buildings and debris.

"You can stay with me as long as it takes."

I carry Carter into the house while grabbing some of their things. Carter lays on the couch with his blanket. I finish helping Emma. I take Carter's things to his room.

"Should I carry him to bed?"

"Please."

I lay with Emma holding her tight. She presses closer into me.

"Don't ever let me go," she whispered.

25

Kallie

I plan on giving Jake a key to my house. I know I am moving soon, but I like the idea of him coming over whenever he wants. I feel a connection to Jake that is incomparable to anything I've ever known. I have never given anyone a key before. I am a little nervous about that.

Jake asked me to come over. I grab Maverick so he can play with Marlee. Jake doesn't mind either, so that is a bonus.

"Kallie, have you ever been to the tractor pulls?"

"No? Does it look like I would go?"

"Good point. I want to take you."

This is the most ridiculous thing I have heard from Jake. Why would anyone want to watch tractors pull other tractors? He grabs my hand, walks me to his truck. He helps me in. I will never understand why tractor pulls are so popular.

It is actually pretty chilly for a summer night. The stars are glowing. . He puts his arm around me. I watch a few tractors pull cars, other tractors, and random stuff.

"I cannot be the only one that thinks this is silly. I hear Jake gasp as one almost goes backwards.

"Did you see that?"

"Yeah, that was pretty cool."

He sees me shivering so hard. He gives me his jacket. I smile. I take his jacket and try to wrap it around both of us. I move closer to him.

"It's fine. I am not that cold." He pauses. "Actually, let's go."

I can't believe I thought a tractor pull was tractors only pulling other tractors. I feel slightly stupid. I do not dare tell Jake that is what I thought tonight would consist of, because he would laugh at me.

I take Maverick home with me. While I lie in my bed, I realize I am missing Jake more than I even realize. Who would have thought I would miss him this much? I have to resist texting him. I don't want to seem desperate. I can't hold back, so I text him. Hey are you still awake? He doesn't respond instead; he calls me; I hesitate to answer. What will I even say to him? I answer. He tells me he can't sleep without me.

"I miss you so much, Jake."

"I will be over in just a moment."

"But Jake, it's is midnight."

"I don't care. I want to be close to you. I cannot fall asleep without you. I don't know what is taking over me."

Is this what real love feels like? Ive never felt this way before. Once Jake arrives, has a key so he lets his self in. I hear him coming up the stairs. My heart starts beating faster. I still get butterflies, even though it's been a few months. I feel him slowly climb into bed. He puts his arms around me. It is like it is meant to be, like it is home. I can be in his arms forever and never complain. I still feel comfortable with him.

He nestles into my neck. I can feel his breath on my skin. I get chills. I start to giggle. because his sounds are so silly. He makes life easy. I could get used to this! I manage to fall asleep so fast in his arms. Is this normal?

As I wake the next morning, I realize this is the first time I fall asleep next to man. I rolled over. The bed was empty. I can't help but wonder where Jake went. Suddenly, I smell something different. It almost smells like sausage and waffles. I don't have anything to make waffles or sausage. I rushed to slide on my slippers. I ran to the kitchen without my robe to see if Jake was there. To my surprise, he was standing over my stove.

"Are you okay? Jake asked.

"I assumed you were gone. I never had a man make me breakfast before."

"I never made breakfast for anyone before, but I would do anything for you."

I feel the mood lighten. My face is now smiling.

Later that day, I can't help but play it back over and over in my mind. I never had a man be so thoughtful. Is this what a relationship is supposed to be like? I call Holden. I need to meet with him because I have so much to talk about. I could really use my best friend right now. I am so torn right now with how I feel. I forgot Holden had already moved. I called him and he tells me this is exactly what a relationship should be like. That gives me comfort. It really sucks not having my best friend around. I can tell Holden feels guilty about not being here for me. I try to convince him I am fine.

I finished packing. Jake, let me put some of my stuff in his garage, since it is still a few weeks away. I didn't want boxes in the listing photos for this house. I put my house on the market finally. I am so scared the new owners will want to close before I move, which means I have nowhere to go. The Realtor told me three people wanted to see it already. I agreed since I was at Jake's today. I just hope someone will put an offer down. I highly doubt it since it is the first day.

I start planning a date to tell Jake my real emotions. I don't want it to be boring or just stupid. I want it to be sweet and romantic. I decided to take him to the lake beach. It is one of our favorite placed to hangout and enjoy the view.

I decided tonight was the perfect night to tell Jake how I feel. I told him I wanted to watch the sunset together at the beach tonight. We sit down in the sand. I stick my toes in the water. It is chilly for August. The sunset is painting the sky orange, yellow, and blue. It is breathtaking. I lay my head on his shoulder. I listen to him talk about how much he will miss this. I look at the side of his face. I take a mental photo of him and the way the sun is hitting his face. I inhale a deep breath. "Jake, I want this forever. I love you with my whole heart." I see him smiling. He turns his head to face me.

"You have no idea how bad I've waited to hear those words from you." He takes my face into his hands. Tonight is so perfect.

I love how his arms feel around my waist. I wish we never had to move from this spot.

"Are you ready to go home?" Jake asks shakily.

I sigh, "Yes but no. I am not ready for tonight to be over."

He helps me stand up. I walk next to him with his hand in mine.

We decided to go back my house. The drive home is full of laughter. I know I will miss this when I do leave for Charleston. I follow Jake to my bedroom. I know I need to have a talk with him about us. I just don't know how to bring it up.

"I move in a few days."

"I know."

"Jake, we do need to talk about it."

"We will always be friends. I do not want to set you back. You finally have your dream job."

I smile at Jake. "It wouldn't be fair to either. Long distance is so hard. You can still visit."

We agree to try to make long distance work, but only time will tell.

I walk into the kitchen; it finally hits me. This will be one of the last times I walk into this kitchen. It will be one of the last times Jake is at this house. It is bittersweet. I take a cup out of the cabinet. I fill it up with water. I take a sip.

Jake is looking sad. "Are you ok Jake?"

"I am thinking about how different it is going to be once you do leave. You are my best friend. I know you have Holden going with you. This past year you have always been here for me Kallie." "I know. I am always here, just like you were for me. It is just distance."

I walk over to Jake. I wrap my arm around his neck. I take in his scent. I kiss his neck. "lets go upstairs." I take him by the hand up the stairs to my bedroom. I gently crawl out my window to sit on the roof. He follows me. Jake sits behinds me. I prop up against him. We sit in silence. The sun is setting. It's so peaceful out here in the country. He kisses my neck.

"Do you want to go back inside?" Jake looks uncomfortable.

"Yeah." I climb back inside. He walks over to the bed.

"Remember the first night you asked me to stay over?"

"It was the night I found out Nash was cheating on me. It isn't something I would forget."

"Yeah, sorry about that." I watch as Jake takes his shirt off. "Come here Kallie." I pause, looking at his body. I slowly walk towards him. He wraps me in his arms.

"I know I will never be Nash. I know you love him."

"Jake, I am happy you will never be Nash. He wasn't always so great to me."

"You should not have to feel less than. He never deserved you Kallie." I instantly look at the ground. How am I supposed to respond to that, after everything that has happened?

Jake places his hand under my chin. He lifts my face up so I am looking at him. "I wish you saw how special you really are. You deserve the world." I am holding back my tears.

"Yeah, I guess you are right. I always give my best to everyone, even if they don't deserve it. I have a big heart."

As it is closer to my moving date, I don't want to leave. Jake is so good to me. I know leaving is the best thing for me. I want to see where my relationship with Jake takes me. I want to make the most of it.

I climb into bed, "Jake, will you kiss me." He pulls me closer to his chest.

"Kallie, you don't have to ask." I feel his mouth on mine. His breathing is labored. Our tongues are swirling together.

He pulls away, "Kallie, you are the best woman I know. I think I am falling for you." I look up at him, "I know, because I am falling for you too Jake. I always want you in my life. Not only have you shown me what love could be like, you shown what a real friend is."

"I know what you deserve, Kallie. Sometimes I wonder if I am the man you need."

"What do you mean?"

"I know how you felt about Nash. I can never be him. I am so different. When I care, I give it my all. You wanted him to support you like you did for him."

"I gave him way too much. With you, it is different. I don't have to try so hard." I bury my face in his chest. He is combing his fingers through my hair. Jake gently kisses the top of my head.

I always thought Nash was the type of man I wanted. The more time I spend with Jake, I realize Nash is everything I despise in a man.

"Jake, I want you."

He pauses, "Like want or like what do you mean?" I climb on top of him.

"I want a relationship. I want us to always be friend. I want you to be the one I call when I have a bad day."

"You kind of already do that, but I understand what you mean. Kallie, I've wanted this since I got to know you." He wraps me in his arms, pulling me to his face. Our mouths meet. I get butterflies when he kisses me. He grabs the back of my nneck,pulling away from my mouth.

"You're my best friend." I pause, "Jake, I am falling so hard for you."

"I know. I feel the same." I take a moment to get my thoughts together.

"Why are you so perfect?"

"I am not perfect. But maybe I am perfect for you, Kallie."

I look into his blue eyes. I can't pull away. I take his hand in mine.

"Yes, I think you are perfect for me. I never knew I needed anyone in my life."

Living with Jake even for the few days we have lived together makes me realize he is perfect for me. He completes me. I thought I fixed my own broken heart. Turns out Jake was the one that helped put it back together. He is my better half. Sometimes, I am my own worst enemy.

Nash brought out the worst in me. Jake brings outs the best in me.

They both we there when I needed someone the most. I still have the guilt of Willow every time I look at Nash. I know time heals everything. I know the wreck wasn't my fault, but I still feel so guilty for killing her. I lay my head on Jake's chest, I take a deep breath. He runs his fingers through my hair. I start to relax a little. He turns on the TV. We both fall asleep.

I wake up looking around. My phone says it is close to 3 am. I turn off the TV. I see something out of my window that catches my eye. Nash is just getting home. I know he saw Jake's truck in the driveway and I hope he doesn't make a scene. I watch him start down Jake's truck as he walks into his house. Nash: really? He is staying again tonight? Me: is it really any of your business? Nash: One day, I will show you I am changing for you and myself. I put my phone on silence before I climb into bed again.

I realize at that moment, Nash and I could never work. He gives me too many mixed signals. I thought after the wreck and him so scared about losing me, he would change. I am not sure he will ever change. We went through such an tragic thing and we are still so back and forth.

26

Nash

I keep seeing Kallie come home smiling. I also keep seeing Jake leaving with a grin on his face. Those two make me sick. If I din't have my own shit, I would be with Kallie.

I am supposed to have my engagement party. I invited Jake because I know he will bring Kallie. That is my chance to get her alone to tell her everything. The thoughts of her and Jake begin to take over my mind. Flashes of red keep coming stronger and stronger. I need to have her. I will have her in the end.

I sent Jake his invitation because I knew Emma wouldn't like the fact I invited Jake. She is really going to be pissed if she finds out I have no plans to marry her. I don't know why she could be so mad. I am the one paying for all of this. It's not like her waitress job can provide for everything she wanted for this event.

I am sad Willow will not be here. Maybe she could be the one to talk some sense into me. Even I can admit, this is fucking insane. Even for me.

What the hell am I doing?

I should just stop this whole thing and get Kallie back. how could ever forgive me after everything I have done? She probably couldn't, but I will try every day to remind her how it used to be and how much I love her. If only she felt the same way.

I am stupid. I can't even call Jake to talk to him about this. I grab a bottle of whiskey and pour 3 fingers. I sip it slowly, thinking about what would Willow say about this. Hell, she would probably slap me. And hard.

27

Kallie

2 months later.

Tonight we are having a "at home date." I do wonder what he has planned. It was almost time for Jake to be home. I grab my keys and drive to Jake's.

Jake pulls me to his chest. "I can't wait to show you what I have planned". He covers my eyes as we walk outside. I can't find the words, I just gasp. "We are having a picnic and a late night swim."

There is a blanket and a bottle of wine next to the pool deck. The pool has flashing lights floating under the water.

"It is beautiful."

I love just at home dates he makes an effort. We sit down on the blanket. Jake sits next to me. "Kallie, I care so much about you." I look deeply into his eyes.

"There are so many things I want to say to you." I take a long pause. "I care about you a lot, as well."

He leans in closer to me. I close my eyes, waiting for him to kiss me. I can feel our mouths touching. "Kallie, I can't be the reason you don't go to Charleston."

I pull away. "Can't we find a way to make this work?" I study his face. It doesn't look reassuring. "I would actually love to find anyway to make it work, but I need one more promise." I nod. "You have to promise me you will go to Charleston."

I giggle. "Of course, I promise Jake."

"Kallie, I — I hate to even ask, but will you go to Nash's engagement party with me?" Jake looks so nervous to even look at me.

"Yeah, I think it could be fun. Obviously, it is completely over between us. I can't even look at him without feeling the guilt. Plus, I would love to be your date, Jake."

I start thinking of my dress options. I have a few favorite ones. Jake starts speaking while pulling me from my thoughts. "What color should we wear?"

"in spite of the bride I am wearing white. I think you would look great in a black blazer with slacks."

I text Holden: I am going to Nash's engagement party with Jake. Holden: Do you think he actually loves her? Me: Nah, I just want to see how bad it is. Holden: What about Jake? Me: That is just a bonus. Holden: That is a terrible idea Kallie. Do not go. I ignore his text.

I know Holden is right. It is a terrible idea to go. Jake is still his friend. I want to support Jake. Nash chose what he wanted in life. I am finally happy with myself. I need to prove I don't need him. I never thought I would be going to Nash's engagement party with Jake. I can't believe Nash is actually marrying the girl he cheated on me with. I slip into my dress. It makes me feel so sexy. It is a white dress, with a deep v neck. It is tight and comes to my mid-thigh. I slip on gold heels. Jake looks equally good. His black blazer is fitting. His black slacks fit in all the right places. "You ready?" "Yes. You look amazing, Jake. I am so glad you didn't bring the truck. This dress makes it impossible to climb." "I do like the dress." Jakes half smile at me.

"This party looks like a fairytale." Jake looks around. "I wonder who paid for all of this?" "Nash and probably Emma's dad." We look around. Let's find a place to sit. Jake looks uncomfortable. I lean into Jake. "It is going to be fine; Nash invited you."

I feel weird being here. Jake is still friends with Nash. I suspect because Nash doesn't know, Jake told me. I don't want to Jake to know I am uncomfortable being here.

"That was the longest party ever." I look up at Jake. "Yeah, the speeches felt like forever long, but they are also lies." We find a standing table for cocktail hour. I am tired of sitting. "Jake, will you dance with me?" "Kallie, no one is dancing." I laugh, "you know I beat to my drum." Jakes laughs. He takes me by the hand. He slowly guides his hand to my lower back. I wrap both hands around his neck. I look up into his eyes. They are so blue today. "You are so special to me Kallie." "you are to me too, Jake." I lay my head on his chest as we dance slowly.

Nash, come up to Jake and I. "So you and Kallie now?" "Yeah, she is my date." Jake is always so careful with words. I smile at Jake and Nash. "It is a lovely party, Nash. I hope you have many years of happiness." I say with the fakest smile. Jake half glances at me. Nash glares at Jake. "You are about crossing the line." Jake stares back at Nash. "We were just leaving."

"So subtle Jake." "They really do deserve each other." I nod. The walk back to Jake's car is silent. I silently get in the car. Jake looks over at me. "You want to come back to my place?" "Yeah Jake. I have clothes in my bag." "Can you keep the dress on a bit longer?" I nod. Jake is so hard to read. I never know what he is thinking. I climb out of his car. I follow him inside. I sit down on his couch. I watch him take off his blazer. His black button down is tight on his muscles. He stands in front of me. "Do you want to dance?" He plays music. "I lift my hand up. "Yes, I would like to dance." I wrap my hands around his neck. He places his hands on my lower back. "You are so beautiful, Kallie." "Thank you." Jake gently kisses my neck. He picks me up. He goes to sit down on the couch. I straddle him. I look deeply into his eyes. I lean in for a kiss.

This feeling is nothing like I ever felt before. You can feel his emotions. Jake makes me feel like I am the only one that matters. I don't feel like I am only here for just sex. Nash only hurt me.

I slowly climb off of him. I need to sit here a moment to catch my breath. Then I realized I need to clean up. He joins in the shower. When I get out of the shower, I get dressed. Are you hungry? I was going to order Chinese food." "Yes, and I love Chinese food." We eat it in bed. Jake gathers noodles in his chopsticks to feed me. I laugh. In a weird way, I actually like that.

I go to the kitchen. I find all the ingredients I am looking for. Jake comes up behinds me. He hugs me from behind. "Good morning, Beautiful." I smile. "Good morning, handsome. I am making breakfast." "Peanut butter chocolate chip waffles.?" "of course." Jake makes everything easy. "Jake, you do know I am moving to South Carolina for work, right?" "Yes, I know. That doesn't mean we can't try before you leave. If it works, there is vacation time and flights always leaving." "Yeah, I just didn't want anyone getting hurt." Jake turns me around to face him. "Kallie, I would never do anything to hurt you. If you want to try, I am all for it. If you don't, I understand too." "Let us see where it takes us, Jake." I wrap my arms around him. His hugs are warm and cozy. He gently kisses my forehead.

It would not be fair to Jake if I started a relationship so soon before the move. I am willing to see how it goes. I am not willing to break his heart. Jake doesn't deserve it.

"I — I — don't want today to be over." Jake stumbles over his words. "I know, I don't either. I do need to go back to my house. You and Marlee can join us." Jake takes a long pause. 6 "I would love that actually.." I look up at him. His eyes are blue like the gulf coast waters.

I have strong emotions towards Jake. He is so good to me. Almost everything I want in a man and relationship. He makes me nervous. I am afraid to fall in love again after Nash broke my heart. I don't want to feel that pain I felt with Nash. It was terrible.

Jake and I take separate cars to my house. "You know can you can stay with me if you want." I nod my head. "I know I can. I just also need to pack my house. I could stay with you after I sell my house." "I would enjoy that, Kallie." I wrap my arms around his waist. Jake kisses the top my head.

Jake lets the dogs go outside to play. They always are so hyper when they first see each other. I sit on the couch. "I am not ready to leave anymore." I lay my head on jakes shoulder. He sighs. "I am not ready either."

I still have a few weeks left. Holden is already gone to South Carolina. Jakes turns on music. "Will you dance with me?" "I will always dance with you, Jake." Jake is my favorite dance partner. He spins me around. I spin back into him. He kisses me. "Jake, I am afraid to feel deeply for you." "I know I scare you. To fall in love again after Nash. I promise I will never hurt you." I take a deep breath. I am scared. He wraps me in his arms. "I know,"

My relationship with Jake is making the move more difficult. I don't want to leave him behind. Only because the distance is hard on anyone. Jake is so charming. He does the small things for me. I really enjoy, like starting my car so it's not so hot. He is kind and understanding.

I never understood when Holden would say, "It is the little things in life that matter the most." I fully understand now. When I see Jake making me coffee or even putting gas in my car, that is how he shows me he cares. When he tickles me and plays around with me, I can feel the love in the air. When he holds me, I can feel how safe we both feel at that moment.

It is the first time someone makes me feel safe. When I am sad and he pulls me to his chest, I feel protected. I always dreamed of how this moment would feel. When he leaves, I feel like half of me is gone. Am I in love or just attached? This doesn't feel like the same love I felt with Nash. I feel comfortable with Jake.

28

Nash

It's disgusting how happy Kallie looks when she is with Jake. I wonder if Emma would want to go out with them. I do miss spending time with Jake. Emma doesn't like when I spend time with anyone else.

Me: wanna go out with Jake and Kallie tonight?

Emma: Hell no.

Well, go figure.

I thought Emma was going to kill Kallie for showing up in white to the engagement party. I think we both know I have no plans on actually marrying Emma, especially when all I want is Kallie. I also know she wants space from me, which is incredibly hard when I live next door to her.

It still hasn't processed that Kallie is actually leaving. I see the for sale sign in her yard. It is a pleasant house. I know it will sell fast. If I didn't love this house so much, I would buy it.

29

Kallie

I attempt to make Jake and me breakfast. The sounds of the fire alarm send Jake running down the stairs. I burnt the biscuits in the oven, and I was so excited to surprise him with a breakfast. I look at Jake as he is laughing hysterically.

"You set the fire alarms off?"

"I burnt breakfast."

I pour our coffee into mugs as he stands by the counter. His laugh makes me start to laugh. I can't believe I actually set the fire alarms off. That is a first for me.

"If your house sells sooner than you thought, you can always move in with Marlee and me. I have a fenced backyard big enough for both dogs."

"I know you do. I just wasn't sure if you were ready for that. I know our relationship is new and we both have strong feelings."

I got an offer on my house. I called Jake, visibly upset. He told me he would be home soon. It all seems so fast. I never thought this house would sell so fast, or everything would come together so quickly to move. Jake comes rushing through the door.

"What is wrong? Why are you crying?"

"I accepted the offer on my house. I have to move out." He wraps his arms around me. "Kallie, you know you always can stay here."

I pull away from him. "Are you sure you are ready for that?"

"I told you I'd do anything for you."

It all seems so quick. I am skeptical because I don't want to mess up our relationship. I need to tell Jake how I feel about him. The real authentic feelings. Maybe he already knows.

I am shocked my house sold so fast. I had two showing. The second person gave me a better offer than the first. I did pick the first person, only because I didn't want to see his house as a rental. I want someone to love this home as much as I do. It is sad knowing it's not my home anymore. I am looking forward to South Carolina and the new opportunities.

I really am going to miss all the memories I've made here. I am excited about the new memories I get to make in Charleston with Holden and hopefully Jake. I know he will visit when he can. Long distance is hard on a new relationship, well any relationship.

I watch Jake at the top of the stairs. I run up them as fast as I can. I watch him slowly take off clothes and climb into bed. I lay next to him with my hand on his chest, I drag my leg over his. I kiss his chest. He holds me tighter. I can tell he is exhausted, I am too. We fall asleep pretty quickly tonight.

The morning sun comes beating down on my window. It is a big day today. I am moving the rest of my stuff into Jake's garage. Closing on my house went faster than I thought it would. I have two weeks until I leave for Charleston. The reality keeps sneaking up that I am leaving so soon. Part of me is ready to leave, the other part wants me to stay. I know logically, I can't stay. I promised Jake I would go, no matter how hard it became for me.

I put my clothes in Jake's room. The closet is pretty empty. All of my clothes fit with his. I place my shoes at the bottom of his closet. I don't have to unpack anything, since Jake has everything I need. I walk past his dresser. Placed on top is a single photo of me. I didn't realize he got a photo of me while at the lake. It is actually a good photo.

Jake doesn't have a lot of photos in his house. Mostly empty walls. I will print off some of my favorites to hang up while he is at work. I work on putting the photos in frames and placing them on the walls. I really like the classic black photo frames against his white walls. It looks classic but not so boring you would overlook them.

I check the time, it still hours before Jake is off work. I decided to go to Coffee and Books for the first time since the accident. I have to face my new reality. I put my shoes on, take a deep breath and walk to my car. I start to dive to Coffee and Books. I am so scared and nervous. I haven't seen Nash since to to tell him we needed space.

My mind starts to race and I feel panic start to wash over me. I find the courage to go inside and order my drink. It doesn't feel the same here without Willow. I slowly walk up to the ordering counter.

"Do you want your usual?"

"Yes, please." I stumble over the yes.

"Can we talk Kallie?"

I nod my head. "Yes, we can."

I patiently wait for my drink. I keep thinking about our last moments together. I start to feel the guilt of leaving town without telling him. I know he cares about me. I needed space and time to process Willow's death. I couldn't do that with him around. Perhaps, I just don't want to admit how much I love Nash even when I am trying so hard to push him away. I keep telling myself that we aren't great for each other.

I walk slowly walked to a table to sit down. Nash could probably tell my leg was hurting. He gives me my drink. It surprised me when he sat down next to me.

"Kallie, I know you are with Jake, but I just need to know that not today but,— maybe someday— we will be together again?"

"Nash, is that a question or a statement?"

"Both. I want to change to be a better person for you. I know you need time to get over the guilt of Willow. It has been 3 months. You must know it wasn't your fault."

I look down, unsure of what to say. I suck my bottom lip in, "Well, I still feel guilty and my feelings are valid."

Nash nods his head, "Yes, they are."

His eyes lock on my face. I still can't look at him, I really don't want him to know, I plan on leaving without saying good bye.

"I should get back to work."

Maybe Nash is right, 3 months later and I still need to attempt to push the guilt away. I need to get my life back without always having to push the guilt away. The accident was exactly that, an accident. I push all the thoughts out of my head. I look around the cafe. It is just Nash and I. I awkwardly smile then look back at my coffee.

I take my coffee to go. In that moment, I just want to run into Jake's arms. I need to know I am doing the right thing. I go straight to Jake's house. Maverick and Marlee are the first to greet me. It is my favorite part of coming home. Jake comes from his kitchen. "I am making coffee, do you want a cup?"

"No, thank you. I went to coffee and Books."

"You look like you need a hug." Jake briskly walks toward me. I fall into his arms. I can't tell him what happen at Coffee and Books, I don't know how he will react. I push all of those thoughts away as I wrap my arms around his back.

"I am fine. I just want a hot bath." Jake walks into his bathroom, drawing me a bath.

"I have some dried lavender to put in it." I slowly walk behind him.

"Thank you." As I slide my shirt off, "Do you want to join me?"

I add some bubbles before I get in the bath. I sit in front of Jake. He helps me lay back onto his chest. "I don't like thinking that you are leaving so soon."

I suck in a deep breath, "I know, but you can always call or visit me or I can come back here."

I try not to get lost in my thoughts. I pick up bubbles in my hands and blow it back at him. I love Jake's laugh, its light and heartwarming. It feels like fresh air after everything we have been through. The water isn't as warm as it should be. I stand up to grab a towel. Jake looks at my leg. "It looks worse than it actually feels these days." His eyes quickly look away as he grabs a towel.

I slip into my pjs and crawl into bed, as Jake goes to let the dogs out. I think I crave normalcy these days. I hated when everyone was so worried about me. It made me never want to answer my phone. Now, I wish I had my friends calling every day. Holden is busy with work and getting the apartment ready. Nash and I are still putting space between us, mostly because of me. I will leave tomorrow. I have a lot on my mind. I also know I need to go to sleep so the drive doesn't take forever. Jake gently slides into bed. I snuggle up to him before I go to bed.

30

Nash

Fuck, she really is gone. Gone to South Carolina and gone to Jake's. I fucked everything up by being with Emma. My hatred for the woman is only growing more each day. I missed my chance with her, and now I am wondering what Jake is doing, now that Kallie is gone.

I wonder if she is at his house and leaving soon since her house has sold. Jake can't avoid me forever, and I plan on starting now. I grab my phone out of my pocket to text Jake.

Has Kallie left?

Jake: no in the morning. She is with me tonight.

I notice he puts his phone on, do not disturb. I would too if I were him. I wouldn't want to waste one second away from. He's smarter than me. I will give him that credit. He hasn't fucked up with her. Now that Emma has less to worry about, she is becoming distant again.

Emma. Such a delicate situation. Part of me wants to run away from everything. To be able to escape and find real happiness. I am tired of forced smiles and hellos.

Everything was so easy with Kallie. I know I have ended things with Emma and soon. I am scared of the backlash and what she might do if she finds out this was my plan.

The big day finally arrived. I get the results of the DNA test I had done. I rip open the letter; I scan the results. I feel half of my heart shattering as I realized I fell into another one of Emma's traps. I lost weeks with Kallie. That was my time to make things right with her. To show her I can be everything she wants me to be.

Red starts to flash as I pour 3 fingers of whiskey. I should have listened when everyone told me to leave this alone, that I should believe Emma that he was not my son.

I look over to the sold sign by Kallie's house. My eyes start burning. Kallie is really gone.

I grab my keys to go to Jake's. If Kallie is still here, that is where she will be.

As I approach Jake's driveway I see her mustang in the driveway. I know they know I am here since my car is so loud.

Jake opens the door. I watch him lead against the door frame with his arms crossed.

"Don't," he says while waving his hand.

I snarl thought my teeth, "You can't stop me."

"Yes, I can."

"Nash, go home." Kallie appears from behind him with Maverick leaving me speachless.

"I needed to see you."

They exchanged glances, "Why?"

"The DNA test came, and it was negative."

They sit there in shock. I don't blame them, I was shocked too when I read the results.

"Oh," Kallie said.

"That's all you have to say?"

"I just don't know what you want us to do with that information."

I give them a shrug.

"Shit, do you wanna come in? I know you really thought Caleb was yours."

"I mean, I did, but I'm relieved since Emma is so crazy."

Jake grabs us a beer, passing them to me. I hand one to Kallie, as she grabs it from me, our hands brush slightly. I see her look away quickly to Jake.

"I don't know why I came here. I just thought it would give me peace to tell someone."

"No, I get it," Jake said.

We finish our beers before Kallie is walking out with Maverick.

"She leaves tomorrow. Can we hang out after?"

"I guess."

I slip my keys out of my pocket. I place my head against the steering wheel.

That is not how I wanted it to go.

I should know she wouldn't leave Jake tonight. While I am not fine with their relationship, I am happy she is happy.

31

Kallie

"Today is the day I leave." I am holding back tears.

Jake looks down at me. "I know, but I made you coffee." I give him a kiss.

"I am not ready to leave."

"Selfishly, I don't want you to either, but I know you want this more than anything."

I grab Maverick's things. I take them to my car. "You ready Maverick?" He wags his tail. I watch him jump into the car. Jake places his hand on my car window.

"Call me when you get there, please?"

I smile. "Thank you for being so supportive."

He puts his hand on my back. "Kallie, I would do anything for you."

I get into my car. Jake shuts the door. I roll down the window. "Remember, I am only a phone call away. Don't cry."

Jake nods. "One last kiss, please?" "

He leans in my car. We kiss one last time. I back out of the driveway. I watch him slowly turn to walk into his house from my mirrors.

I call Jake. "I am almost at my new apartment."

"I miss you like crazy, Kallie."

"I miss you too, Jake. I do have to go. I have to call Holden."

I finally found a parking spot. Holden is waiting for me. "Are you ready to see your new apartment?"

This apartment is a dream. The big open windows let in the sunlight. The sheer curtains are more for aesthetics. We place the couch where you can see the ocean and the TV. The Kitchen faces to the living room. The floors are light brown. Down the hall are two bedrooms. A bathroom at the end of the hall. My bedroom has access to the walk out balcony. Holden can't sleep if there is so much light. I got pretty lucky.

"I am so excited to get patio furniture so we can sit outside. We can read, work on manuscripts. I love this apartment." I tell Holden.

Holden looks at me, smiling, "I knew you would! Now let's go see the city." I take the stairs down to the parking garage. "How is the traffic from here to work?"

"I was lucky enough to find a beach from apartment within 10 minutes from work."

"I start on Tuesday; I didn't want to take too much time off." I realistically took 3 days off. I left on Thursday, unpacked Friday and Monday. I didn't want to have too much traffic on my way down.

Holden keeps driving. "I want to show you my new favorite restaurant."

"Ok, I am hungry."

"It even has rooftop seating. You can eat. At night it turns into a bar. The food is amazing." "Do they have wings?"

"Wings and pasta. I know you would love this place. Do you want to sit on the rooftop?" This place is amazing. The rooftop over looks the ocean for miles. It's a block from the beach. I ordered Carolina Wings.

"What are Carolina wings?"

"It's a mustard-based bbq sauce. It is actually pretty good."

"I will try it."

I think this is my new favorite place too. "Are you excited about seeing your new office?"

"Yes, I am also so nervous. What if my editing style is too different?"

"You would not have even been offered the new job if they didn't think you would be great at it. We don't have to share an office like we did when we were interns."

"Oh, I get my own?"

"We both do."

I finally get to my bedroom the way I like it. I have white curtains for the windows. I decided on gold and navy decorations for my walls. I place a navy rug under my bed. I decided on floating shelves for photos and my favorite books. I place them next to my bed. I find 3 of my favorite book and 2 photos. I have my favorite photo of Jake and me from the day on the river. The other photo is of Holden and me from our first day as interns. I went with a white bed set. I could not decide one, so I went with plain to let my accents make a statement.

Tomorrow is my first day at work. I am so nervous and excited. I am second guessing myself; I feel like I need more confidence in my skills. I only have two years of experience. I look at myself in the mirror. My skin is glowing. I think I look at the art. I open my bedroom door. The first thing I smell is coffee.

I come out of my bedroom. "Holden, do I look good on my first day?"

I decided to wear my black pencil skirt, black heels and a navy-blue blouse. It is actually pretty comfortable. "Yes, you look fine. Do you need help to bring anything?"

"Not today. I am just going to bring my laptop, small office supplies, and maybe a photo. They all can fit into my bag."

"Maybe you should get a new bag? You have had that one forever."

"I know, but it's simple, with a lot of pockets and can hold everything I need.

Holden decided to drive us. It is a relief. I didn't want to get lost. The building is beautiful. First thing I notice is the huge windows. "Wow, this building is huge and fancy."

"It's all windows, and our offices overlook the beach."

We take the elevator to the 10th floor

. "You weren't kidding. This place just screams elegant."

The reception area is all white. Even the orchids have white flowers. A beautiful chandelier; It's bright and airy.

"Here is your office and mine is right next door. So, if you need anything."

"Ok great." I admire my view from the window. I have an orchid in the window. I can see the horizon where the water and sky meet. My desk is white. It's big enough for my desktop and my laptop. I have a gold paper sorter. I will label those for read, need to read, and yes/no piles. My chair is black and leather. It smells like leather. I have a simple white bookcase. My office looks so empty currently. I make a list of things I need and want to bring to the office. I need to go shopping after work.

There is a knock on my door. "Come in."

"Hi, I am Charles. I am your new boss. I have your first manuscript. Edit and send it back to me."

"Yes, sir." He is charming. "You have 5-7 days, depending on the length, to edit one and get it back to me. Please return them in the folders with the correct name. Do you have any questions?"

"No, not at this moment."

"Ok, well, Holden is next door. They set your email up. You will see my emails and the secretary's emails. If you have any questions, please don't hesitate. Lunch break is from 12 to 1." "Perfect."

Holden: good luck today. You got this. Thanks I text him back. I put my phone in the desk drawer. I can only imagine Jake is going to text or call me. I can't be distracted on my first day of work. I look at the manuscripts. These are going to take forever. They are at least 500 pages. I grab my red pen and a highlighter. There will be a lot of long nights on my balcony, working. Maybe it is a good thing I left Iowa. I don't have any time for distractions or drama.

I tried to call Jake. He barely answers his phone anymore. That isn't Jake. I hear my phone vibrate in my desk. Jake: sorry I never answer, I am so busy with work. Me: It's ok Jake. Can you call me tonight?

"Are you ready to go?"

"yeah, I just need to grab my laptop. I also need to go shopping when I get home from my office."

"Ok do you want me to come with you?"

"Only if you want. My office is too blank. I need something to make it feel cozier."

I find a cute, simple gold stapler. I grab more red pens, white out, and post-it notes. I find these cute woven baskets to hold all my over supply of pens and papers. I need to find another paper shelf. I need a memo board and a calendar to stay on track.

I am ready for my second day of work. I place a few of my favorite books on my bookshelf with a photo of Holden and me. On the shelf under that, I place a photo of Jake next to my printer. I place my baskets on the bottom shelf. I throw my extra pens and highlighters in one basket. The second basket holds extra paper. My third basket is empty. I place my memo board on the wall next to me. It will be easy to stick post-it notes on it. My calendar is right under my memo board. It is easy access to write due dates and when I received the manuscript. My office is the way I want it. It doesn't look so white now. I sit down in my chair. I start to work. I put my phone in my drawer. Jake is calling. "Hey Jake, I am at work."

"Oh sorry. I just wanted to hear your voice; will you call me when you get off?"

"Yeah, but I do have to go." I hang up. I start to get to work.

"Hey Kallie, have you met Charles?"

"Yes, why?"

"He is the editor in chief. He will be coming to your office today to check in on you." "Thanks Holden."

"Hello, I am Charles. Well, if you need anything, let me know I can do a bulk order for you."

"Thanks, I should place an order for Ink. Other than that, I don't need anything."

I need to call Jake. He probably just wants to hear about my day. I get into my car. I call Jake on my way home.

"Hey Kallie."

"Hey, I am off work. Is now a bad time?"

"No, not at all. How is work going?"

"The usual. I am more interested in how your job is going." "I have my office. The window overlooks the ocean. It's all white. Holden's office is next door to mine."

"Oh, is he liking the job, too?"

"Yes, so we do the same thing. We have to edit manuscripts, then we send it back to the publisher. Before copy writing."

I met the editor in editor-in-chief the copy writing. The pay is incredible, and the benefits are equally great."

"That does sound good. I do miss you."

"I miss you too, Jake."

"I wish we could talk more."

"I know, I am so busy and the time difference also makes it difficult."

"I have vacation time coming up. Can I see you soon?" "I need to talk to Holden, but I would like that."

If Jake does want to visit soon; I do need to see if Holden would be alright with it. I feel like we spend so much time at work and even when we are home, we are working. He shouldn't mind. I can't take off work, I don't have vacation even if I did, I would fall so far behind at work. I walk to Holden's bedroom. I lightly knock. "Come in Kallie." I go to sit on his bed next to him. "Sorry to bother you, but Jake wants to come Visit. Would you be ok with him staying here?" "This is your home too. You can bring whoever you want here.

"I know. I just thought you would be uncomfortable with him here."

Holden is laughing. "I think I can handle it. Just don't be too loud. That would make me uncomfortable."

I call Jake. "Can you come in like two weeks?"

"Of course I can."

"Ok, I will see you soon then." I can't help but to smile. I feel the butterflies in my stomach. I hope this goes great.

The sun is starting to set. I walk out onto my balcony. I plug in the outside string lights. I grab my laptop and my last manuscript for the week. I admire the waves crashing onto the shore. I really don't want to work. I rather be out there playing. I get started on my laptop. I read the title page. This one sound interesting. The last three weren't my favorite reads. That is probably the worst part of my job. Reading topics that I have no interest in.

"Hey, mind if I work out here too?"

"Sure, sit down. I am just trying to edit this last one before tomorrow." I take a deep breath. I know Holden will be honest with me. I have to make sure.

"Holden, am I stupid for thinking long distance can work?"

"Stupid no, ambitious yes. I guess, in theory, it could work."

"I guess it takes a lot more communication and trust."

"Do you trust Jake?"

"Oh, absolutely." I smile at Holden. "Let's get to work. We have a lot to do. I am glad I get to have my best friend with me."

"Hey, I am going to leave for coffee. Want anything Holden?"

"No, I am fine." I open the door. Jake is standing there.

"Surprise! I couldn't wait any longer. I needed to see you."

"I am so happy to see you Jake!" he picks me up. I wrap my legs around his waist and my arm around his neck. I kiss his neck gently.

"I have missed you so much Kallie. You have no idea."

"I think I have a good idea." He walks into the apartment. I tell him where my bedroom is. He lays me down on the bed. I pull him with me. I quickly take his shirt off. Jake is kissing my neck. "Jake, your phone is ringing." I look at the screen.

"How did you know where my apartment was?"

Jake smiles, "I called Holden. He helped me plan this."

"That explains everything."

Jake turns to me. "Any day I get to spend with you is worth it."

"Lets go to the beach!" we walk down the shoreline, holding hands.

"The water feels nice."

I look at the water. "Yeah, the sand gets so hot it burns my feet."

Jake takes me by surprise. He picks up me and walks into the water. He throws in me. "Not nice, Jake!" Another wave is coming. I jump onto Jake's back. Now you can't get me. He takes a deep breath, so do I. He jumps into the wave.

"I wish I was tall enough to do that. I have to stand on my tippy toes and then jump. It makes me legs hurt."

"I got you. Hold on tight."

A bigger wave comes. He grabs tighter to my thighs. The waves take us both, crashing on top of us. "You OK Kallie?"

"Yeah, just a mouthful of water."

He go back to the shore. I lay out an over sized beach towel. "I am having a great time here."

"I knew you would like Charleston." Jake sits beside me. I lay back trying to dry off a bit more. Jake lays on his side facing me. "I am burning. Do you want to walk back yet?"

I huff, "No because that means our day together is almost over." He kisses my forehead.

"I will be back soon."

We walk back to the apartment. "This sand is so hot." I watch Jake run from the sand. I start laughing. "Did that help?"

"Hell no, my feet are still hurting."

I run cool water in the shower. "Jake, stick your feet in."

"That does make it feel better." I should have warned Jake the sand here gets so hot. He takes me in his arms.

"Today has been the best days in a while, Kallie."

I hate Jake has to go back to Iowa. I haven't had this much fun with anyone in a while. Holden is my best friend, but it is different with him. I do have fun with Holden.

"Are you ready to go?"

"Yes, and no." I wrap my arms around him.

"Only a few more week." He kisses. I take him to the airport. The silence is loud.

I walk with him. I kiss him goodbye. I look into his eyes. They are even more blue. I can see him holding back tears. I wave bye and walk back to my car. I hope one day, he will be able to move here.

I am crying by the time I make it back to the apartment. "Kallie, are you ok?" I shake my head as Holden walks to me. "I just miss Jake."

"Come watch a movie with me. It might take your mind off of Jake. Holden brings me water from the kitchen. "Drink this." I take the water.

"What movie are we watching?"

"This terrible horror movie I found. It's so bad it's actually funny."

I laugh. "I need to laugh."

"Have you talked to Charles about leaving for Iowa?" Holden asked.

"I sent him an email." I said.

"I think we actually get labor day off."
Holden said.

I cannot wait to go back home to visit Jake. I have thought about this day since he left. I am nervous. I pace on my balcony, thinking of what to pack. I got the email back from Charles. I do have labor day off. I also should work a little on editing since it is an extra day off work. I grab my work bag. I throw my pens, folders and laptop and charger into my bag. I don't need a lot for my trip.

32

Nash

Fuck, she really left for South Carolina. Kallie didn't even say bye.

33

Kallie

6 months later.

It feels weird being home. I am so excited to see Jake. I just landed at the airport. I have worked so hard to push Nash out of my thoughts. Part of me wonders if I will run into him. I can't help but to wonder if I am making the right choices.

I love being in South Carolina. I love Jake. I cannot shake Nash from my thoughts. Being back home is a curse, and I don't like it.

"Hey Jake!" My voice is too high pitched. I didn't realize how much I missed him. He takes me into his arms. I bury my head in his chest. He smells really good.

"Are you ready to go home? Let me take your bags."

I follow Jake to his truck. He put my things in the backseat before helping me climb in. He takes my hand before he starts the truck. "I have missed you, too."

I can tell something is off with Jake. It is too silent in the truck. I just don't know how to ask if it is the distance.

I stay quiet at his house. I can't it the silence anymore. It's the loud silences that seems to get louder with every passing minute.

"What is wrong, Jake? You have barely spoken a word since I got home."

"I am just worried you will run into Nash while here. He broke off his engagement. I just don't want to lose you again." I nod and sit quietly.

I know how this goes. Any inconvenience with Nash, he always hits me up. Jake and Nash are still friends; he knows I am here this weekend.

I bring my bags into Jake's house. Jake is still being quiet.

"Jake, stop. I didn't come here for you to act this way. We only have a weekend."

"I know. I am sorry. I want to make the most of it."

I wrap my arms around him. I take in his scent. He still smells go nice. I miss him holding me. I care so deeply for Jake. It is also so different since I came back home.

I hear my phone buzzing on the counter. Jake slowly drops his arms from me. I got to check my phone. Of course it is Nash.

Nash: Hey.

Me: What do you want from me?

Nash: I just want you to be happy.

Me: Then let me be happy.

Nash: Meet me tomorrow morning at Coffee and Books?

I don't know what to say. My mind is racing with the what if. I take a moment before I text him back.

Me: I can't.

I throw my phone back on the counter. Jake walks up behind me. "Kallie, what is wrong?"

I turn to face him"Nash wants me to meet him. I told him I can't. I don't have anything to say to him." I see concern in his face.

"If you want to, you can see him. I do trust you Kallie."

"I know you do. What could he possibly have to say to me?"

We decide to go to Coffee and Books. I desperately need coffee. I am holding Jake's hand when we walk in. He moves his arm around me, pulling me closer to his side. Jakes order from us as I find a place to sit. I just want to enjoy a simple conversation that doesn't involve Nash. I find a free table and sit down. I look up. Nash is standing in front of me. I stand up. I feel Jake standing behind me.

"Kallie, I told you I would never give up on us. I love you Kallie." I roll my eyes.

"Nash, you cannot do this here."

"I don't care. I love you."

"No you don't. You loved the convince of me!" Jake places his hand on the small of my back. "Nash you have already crossed this line once. Leave her alone."

Nash grumbles, "You can't make her happy the way I can." Jake is irritated now.

"Obviously you can't. You broke her heart."

I locked my eyes on Nash. Nash's face is turning red. He looks sweaty. His eyes are full of rage. It is scaring me. I take a step back. I look at Jake. He looks angry, but not as angry as Nash. Nash takes a swing. His fist collides with Jake's face. Jake's face is now red. Jake punches Nash. Nash grabs Jake by the neck. I watch him throw Jake to the ground. Jake hits the chair as he is falling. Nash gets on top of him, starts punching him.

"Stop!" I yell. Nash keeps repeatedly punching Jake.

I run over to Nash, trying to push him off of Jake. His fist hits against my face. Nash jumps off Jake.

"Oh my God, Kallie. I didn't mean to hit you. Let me see."

"Get away from me, Nash." I try to get away from Nash. I can hear him following me.

"Kallie, wait." I hear Jake coming behind me. "Nash, you need to leave her alone."

Jake slams the car door in Nash's face. He takes my face in his hands. "Let me see how bad it is." He takes off his shirt to hold pressure on my lip.

"I can't believe he hit me."

"He crossed the line Kallie."

I watch Jake follow me inside his house. I have never seen him angry before.

"I never would have texted him back if I knew he would go this far."

"It's not your fault. He knew what he was doing. He knows we are together." I wrap my arms around myself. Jake rushes to me.

"Kallie, I promise this isn't your fault. He is toxic and isn't good for anyone. You know this."

"Jake, your lip is bleeding."

I walk with Jake to the bathroom. I help him clean the blood off his lip and face. Jake notices blood on his shirt. His face is red from anger. He takes off his shirt, throws it at the wall.

"Kallie, you don't have to clean up the blood. I got it." I continue to hold pressure on his nose.

"Looks like you may have a black eye."

I get Jake an ice pack from the kitchen and wrap it in a kitchen towel. I place it in Jake's eye. He winces a little. "It should help."

Jake doesn't take long to calm down. Seeing Jake angry for the first time was shocking. He is so chill, I never expected to see a fight. I am a little taken back by it. They put me in a tough place. I don't like seeing him with busted knuckles or lip. I definitely do not like seeing Jake and Nash fight over something so stupid. I am almost positive Nash broke Jake's nose.

I do know Nash isn't good for me. He needs to change a lot before I could even see him again. I didn't deserve how he treated me. It is all a game to him. This weekend was supposed to be about me and Jake. Jake also needs to have a talk with Nash about respecting the boundaries.

I am so sorry Kallie. I didn't know it was you pulling me off, Jake. I would never hit you. I blacked out from the rage. Turn off my phone. I am so angry with Nash. I was the only other person there. He had to know it was me pulling him off Jake.

I sit on the couch. Jake sits next to me. I curl up with him. "What an eventful first day." He huffs. I don't even know why he still tries." "He will never change. Better question. Why are you still friend with him?" I search his face for an answer, since he refuses to say anything.

I go to the kitchen for water. I decided to text Nash back. I will meet you at coffee and Books at 7 am sharp.

"Jake, I need to meet with Nash to tell him I am serious about him leaving me alone."

"OK, I hope he listens to you."

"I leave Sunday, so it shouldn't be a problem."

I wake up earlier than Jake. I grab one of Jake's shirts to wear. I leave for Coffee and Books. Nash is already here with my order. I smile at him and take my drink.

"Kallie, what do I have to do to get you back in my life?" I take a sip of my coffee.

"Nothing. There is nothing you can do, Nash. I can never forgive you for all the mess you made." I stand up, ready to walk out. "Stay away from Jake." I demand.

I get back to Jake's house. I pull out my laptop. I have a manuscript that I need to start on. I start to edit it. I hear Jake walking behind me.

"Good morning, beautiful." I stand up and give him a kiss. I wrap my hand around his neck.

"Good morning, handsome."

"Do you have a lot of work to do?"

"I am just editing what I can today. Tomorrow with the flights I can edit a lot more. So depends on what a lot means."

He chuckles. "I have a big day planned for us."

I lean my head back and take a deep breath. Why did I even say I will work while I am here?

I can't wait to have a whole day with Jake. I watch him set up for our first event. Pizza and paint at home. "I bought everything we need to have quality time together." He draws the curtains down. I sit with Jake on the floor.

"What are we painting?"

"I got stencils because we aren't artist."

I laugh. I dropped the pizza sauce on the canvas.

Jake laughs. "I forgot how messy you are."

I laugh. I clean off my canvas and start painting. I picked blues and golds. It will look so good in my bedroom. As I am almost finished, I look at Jake's. He taps my nose with his paintbrush. I laugh, he laughs. He only picked black paint.

"It will look good anywhere I put it, since it is black."

He lays back on the floor. He looks so good. I lay beside him. He wraps his arm around me to pull him closer to me.

"I am not ready for this weekend to be over." He combs his fingers in my hair.

"You make me happy Jake." I see a little smile. "What else are we doing today?"

"Well, I got your favorite movie and candy. I thought it would be nice and relaxing because you leave. I wanted to spend quality time."

"I do like that." I whisper.

"Also, there are fireworks over the river tonight on Labor Day."

It has always been the small things with Jake. Sometimes, I feel like the small things do not add up to the big thing I crave. I almost think something is missing.

Jake made a fort in the living room. Of course, Marlee comes to join us. It is hard to watch the movie when I can't stop looking at Jake shirtless. His muscles tighten every time he grabs more popcorn. I move closer to him. I face him. Jake sits up on his arm. He starts to tickle me. I grab a pillow and hit him with it. He gently hits me back. He leans his head back, laughing.

"This is great Kallie."

He slowly leans in for a kiss. His hand is in my hair. The other hand is holding mine. He lays me back slowly, moving on top of me. Jake starts kissing me hard. I can't catch my breath. I place my hands on his chest. I need to be close to him. I wait for him to take off my shirt. He slowly starts kissing and licking my neck. I look into his icy blue eyes. Jake begins to take off my shirt. He pulls away from me.

. "Kallie, I want to, but I can't."

I frown. "Why?"

"Because it doesn't feel right. After everything that has happened this weekend."

I nod slowly. "Okay, can we cuddle?"

"That we can do."

I place my head on Jake's chest. I listen to his heartbeat. I try to focus on the movie. I can't stop admiring him. I gently caress his side with my fingertips. His fingers run through my hair. I miss moments like this the most. I hate living so far from Jake.

It is almost time for the fireworks. Jake lays out a blanket for us to sit on in the back of his truck. He wraps his arms around my lower back. I lead my head on his shoulder. It is pretty dark next to the water. The bright lights from the fireworks light up his face. He looks at me.

"I love how excited you get for small things in life Kallie."

"It is the small things that make up the bigger parts of life, I believe."

Jake takes me to the airport. He hugs me goodbye. "I will see you soon." I kiss him one last time. I check my phone for the time.

"I can't miss my flight. I will see you soon." His arms drop from my waist.

I slide my phone into my back pocket. Once I fill a buzz, I pull it out. Nash: Have a pleasant flight. Don't work too hard. Me: I always work hard or at least try. And I will. Is this Nash trying to show me he can change and be a friend? He didn't treat Jake well this weekend. That is supposed to be his best friend. I shake those thought out of my head. It is only a two hours and 25 minute flight back to Charleston. I was lucky enough to find a nonstop flight. So I will work while flying back home.

I board the plane. My mind keeps racing between the manuscript I am reading and the Jake/Nash situation. I think I should cut them both off. I focus harder on my screen. I really should have printed the manuscript. I didn't want to have 350 pages to keep up with. I am a quarter of the way through my editing when the plane is getting ready to descend. I close my laptop.

When I get to the airport, I text Holden. I am almost off the plane. Holden is waiting for me with coffee in hand. "Thank you. I needed this."

"I figured. I can't wait to hear all about your trip."

I quickly start walking to keep up with Holden. I get into his car before I start telling him everything. I start by telling him how Jake was weird all weekend. Then I told him about Nash. "Do you love him?"

"Holden, which him are you referring to?"

He chuckles. "Either or both?"

I smirk and look at him. "Is it bad I am entertaining the idea Nash and I could be together again if he would just change?"

Holden glances back at me. "I like to think anything is possible. I do feel like Nash would have a lot of change. Is it bad? No. Not really. I know you still love him."

I sigh. "Yeah, but I just don't know if I can trust him. He has to rebuild that. He went to Jake's house just to speak to me."

Holden laughs. "He is brave. I give him that."

"Jake is nice and great, but this weekend was weird. I almost feel like something is missing when I am with him."

I look out the window. We are almost home.

I just want to sink into my bed. Forget about the weekend from hell. I text Jake to tell him I made it home. I stare at my ceiling thinking reflecting about the weekend. I should finish my work before tomorrow, I don't feel motivated.

I grab my phone. Me: Hey, I made it back to Charleston. It was a pleasant flight. Nash: I'm glad. Thanks for letting me know. I hope to hear from you soon. I smile at my phone. I take a photo of me laying in my bed to send to Nash. He sends one back of him in his bed. I save it on my phone. I decide to call Nash.

"We need some rules if we want to be friend."

"Alright."

"1. Stay away from Jake. 2. Respect the boundaries of me wanting space. 3. You have to show me you are changing and I can trust you or we are done."

"I can do all of that. I will show you Kallie."

I hang up with Nash. I think this could be good. I miss him. I miss how we used to do things together. I crave him still. I want to believe he is changing. This is more complicated than it has to be. I haven't spoken to Jake since I told him I was home. I have nothing to say to him. I need a hug.

"Holden, I need a hug."

He wraps his arms around me. "It is going to be okay, Kallie, I promise."

I pull away. "You're right. I need to end things officially with Jake."

34

Nash

I heard Kallie is home visiting Jake. I just wanted to see her. I knew she would be glowing from the sun and happiness. I wish Willow could see her now. She is much different from the pale freckled face woman we knew and loved. Something about her seems different.

Seeing her today made me regret the past year. I knew I needed to be back in her life. I am determined to show her how great of a man I am. I spent the last six months changing for the better. I gave up drinking all to focus on myself and making me a better person. I hope she knows that. I pray she can see the changes in me.

I probably scared her. I didn't mean to hurt her or to hurt Jake. Seeing them together stings.

I will not stop. I can't stop.

35

Kallie

I go with Holden to work. My office still has photos of Jake on the shelves. I ignore those and start to work on my manuscripts. By the time lunch is here, I only want coffee. It is hard to focus when I have too much on my mind.

I decided to walk to the coffee shop since Holden drove today. The man in front of me sounds too familiar. I look down at my phone to see if Jake has texted me. He hasn't. As I walk up to the counter to order my drink, the cashier smiles at me, "that guy ordered and paid for your drink." I smile at the cashier with a confused look on my face. I look over to see who paid for my drink. Nash is standing at the pickup counter.

I slowly walk over to him. "What are you doing here?"

"You never gave me the chance to tell you anything when you can to Iowa." Nash is smirking.

"I have to get back to the office. Can you call me later to explain?"

"Yes."

I rush back to work, pacing in Holden's office. I tell him about Nash being here and he equally looks puzzled. I finally get my thoughts together. I sit in the chair across from Holden. "Kallie, I don't think it is a bad thing he is here." I glance at the clock.

"My break is over. I told him to call me after work." I keep waiting for my phone to vibrate. I want to know why Nash is in Charleston and what didn't he tell me. I make small edits to the manuscript, I place a sticky note to come back to this later.

The car ride home is silent. Nash didn't text me. Jake still hasn't texted me. I start to think I liked Jake because he was convenient. When we got home, I quickly changed into my comfy pajamas and went out to the balcony. After a few moments alone, I hear Holden opening the sliding door.

"You alright, Kallie?" Holden hands me a cup of coffee.

"I don't know." I process my thoughts. I watch Holden nod slowly, like he is thinking of what to say.

"I know. My heart belongs to Nash. I feel guilty because Jake was there after the wreck and the recovery time." I take a sip of my coffee.

"So was I, Kallie."

"Yeah, but you are my best friend. It is different because I can be open and honest with you."

It is amazing how Holden always seems to know what I am thinking. I am so grateful to have a friend like him. We sit in silence, watching the waves break on the shore. I reflect on what Holden said. I don't owe anyone anything. I still have days where I do feel like I owe some kind of loyalty to Jake. After everything we went through; he was still here for me.

My phone ringing breaks me from my thoughts. I grab my phone and walk into my bedroom before I answer.

"I was wondering when you were going to call."

"I got busy at work. I was going to call you."

"What did you want to tell me?"

"I rather do it in person. Can I see you soon?"

"Yes, tomorrow about 6?" After I wait for Nash to confirm, I hang up the phone.

I have to call Jake, or maybe text him.

Me: we should talk soon. Jake: alright.

I wasn't expecting Jake to call me right away. I answer the phone and he notices the change in my voice.

"Are you alright Kallie?"

"Yes, I think we should just be a friend."

"I figured it was coming. Can we be friends?"

"Yes, I will always be here for you."

I hang up with Jake. I think it went well. I start to feel guilty. Maybe I shouldn't have done it that way, but it's hard when we are so far apart. I look around my bedroom. I start picking up my dirty laundry to place in the hamper. Maybe I will take Maverick to the beach. I change into my swimsuit. I throw shorts and shirt over. I grab his leash. He comes running from behind me. "Let's go play in the water."

"Holden, want to go to the beach with us?"

"No, I think I am going to rest. I am exhausted."

We walk down to the shore. Maverick dives headfirst into the waves. I watch him try to bite the waves crashing. He is a goofy dog living his best life. The sunshine feels great on my face. Luckily it is still warm for September. The Atlantic waters are usually chilly, even in the summer. Luckily, the sand isn't too hot to burn my feet or his paws.

Maverick starts to get tired. I walk him back to the shore to lie on the sand. I forgot a towel per usual. I check my phone for the time. I have this instinct to call Nash. He picks up on the first ring.

"Where are you, Kallie?"

"I am at the beach with Maverick. I was thinking about you, so I called to hear your voice."

"I miss you too. I actually have to go."

I sigh as I hang up the phone. I need water. I decided to go back to my apartment. I walk into my apartment. Holden looks nervous.

"Everything fine?" I asked him.

"Actually, I think you should go into your room."

I have a puzzled look on my face as I hurry to my room. Nash is standing there with white roses. I run to jump into his arms. I feel his warm arms rubbing my back.

"What? I can't believe you are here."

He smiles. "Holden helped me set it up."

"Really?" I wrap my arms around his neck. "I am so happy you are here."

"Me too."

I miss this man more than I could ever imagine. I am so happy he is here and Holden helped Nash set this up. I know I don't need Holden's approval but it makes me feel better about Nash and me. Nash sits down on my bed never letting go of me. I feel like at this moment, he is the only thing that matters.

"I am never letting you go again."

I lean my head on his. "Promise?"

"As long as you have me," Nash whispers.

"Our past is a part of our story. There are some things I wish I could change, but I can't. I want to show you I am different now, Kallie. You make me want to be a better person."

"I know, Nash, we have just been through a lot. And I mean a lot." I breathe in as I think of what I want to say.

"So, what did you want to tell me at the coffee shop?" I look down at my feet.

"I actually live here now. After you left, I asked my job to relocate me."

I look at Nash with a puzzled look.

"I wanted a change, and I needed to get away from everything that reminded me of Willow."

I wrap my arms around his neck. I can see how it would be hard for Nash to constantly have to work his job, the coffee shop, and be reminded every day of her. I don't understand how he can look at me and not be reminded of that night I crashed us into a tree.

I start to think of things for us to do today. All I want to do is with Nash. I would be content sitting in my room with him all day. We walk out onto my balcony. He admires the view. I see him looking over at me.

"Do you want to take a walk on the shore?"

I glance back at him. "Yes."

I take his hand as we walk down to the beach. The waves lapping over our feet as we walk. I see a jellyfish.

"Have you ever held a jellyfish?" I grab it for him to touch it.

Nash looks at me weird, "will it sting me?"

I laugh, "no these are harmless."

I place it in his hands gently. He makes a face.

"It so weird feeling."

I make sure the jellyfish will be able to make its way back the deep in the ocean. I sit down in the sand where the water will only reach my feet. It's pretty chilly with the wind and water.

Nash wraps his arms around me. "You seem cold."

I nod my head. I don't feel like words are necessary at this moment. I lay my head on his shoulder, admiring the sun going down over the horizon. It always amazes me how the sky can turn such beautiful shades of orange and blues.

I look over at his face. I see a small smile. "I have missed this Kallie more than you could ever know."

A smile appears on my face now, "me too, Nash."

We sit in silence. Nash stands up. He reaches down for my hand to help me up. He wraps his arms around me. "I promise, I will never let you go." Before I could stop myself, I let out what I can't stop thinking.

"If you wanted a fresh start, why are you here with me? How can you look at me and not see Willow's killer?"

"You didn't kill her. The drunk drive that went into your lane did! That's how Kallie." I cut my eyes back to the ocean. "I am sorry." I have tried so hard to push that behind me, somehow, it is in the back of my mind. I try not to change the good time or the good moods. I grab Nash's hand.

"Do you want to come back to my room?"

"No, I want to take this slow and do it right this time."

Nash walks me back to my apartment before he leaves.

"Holden, thank you." I smile.

"He told you?"

"Of course he did. I also asked how he knew where my apartment was."

"I promised I would keep it a secret. I didn't know much more than you did."

"I didn't know you were friends."

"Not exactly, mostly because of you."

I sit down at the bar. Holden gives me a glass of water. I can't stop smiling at him.

"He said he wants to go slow and do it right this time."

"I think that is a great idea. He is already showing he can change."

"I am still not convenience he has changed a lot."

At this moment, I am reminded of how good of a friend Holden is to me. He puts his own feelings aside about me and Nash. He helped Nash. Never in my life did I think those words could come out of my mouth.

Maybe Nash hasn't changed much, but the way he is trying to show me how much he is trying to be a better person. It almost makes me want to give him a real second chance. He wants to go slow. There was nothing slow about Nash before everything happened. Why does he suddenly want to go slow? I wonder what Jake knows. I can't exactly ask him about this.

I lay in my bed looking out the windows. It's too dark to see the ocean. I crack the glass door so I can listen to the waves crashing on the shore. I start to reflect on the last year of my life. The ups, the downs, the middles. Since I have met Nash, my life has been full of mostly ups and downs. How can I even trust him after everything? I think I am stupid for even giving this a second thought. My heart says yes, while my head is screaming, "This is a terrible idea!"

I look at the clock, when I realize I need to sleep or tomorrow will be terrible. As I close my eyes, I hear my phone ding. I miss you. I half smile as I text Nash back. I miss you too. He sends me an address. I debate if I want to go to it.

I decided to go. I get dressed quickly. I quietly sneak out of the apartment without waking up Holden. As I start to drive to the address, I start to get butterflies. By the time I make it, it is super dark and pouring down rain. I start to have flashbacks from the night I wrecked Willow's car. I pull over and take several deep breaths before I feel fine to drive again.

36

Kallie

I feel the rain pouring off my skin. I grab Nash's arm before he can turn away. I admire his face.

"It has always been you, Nash." He looks at me in disbelief. "Nash, I always loved you."

He wraps his arms around my back. I can smell a faint hint of his cologne. The rain is beating down on us. He slowly picks me up. I wrap my legs around him.

"Kallie, I love you so much."

The rain is dripping from his hair onto my face. The street light is making the water glow. I push his hair out of his face so I can look into his eyes. The tension is thick between us. I place my forehead against his, I slowly place my hands on the sides of his face. I kiss him while feeling our tongues swirl against each other. The rain is coming down harder now. I push my body closer to his.

"I don't ever want to be separated from you again," Nash whispered into my mouth.

"Forever." I mumbled back while still kissing him.

Nash gently places me down. "Come on." He grabs me by the hand as we walk side by side to his apartment. Once we are inside, he gives me the blue shirt from when we first met. I slip off my wet clothes.

"I've always liked this shirt on you." I said.

"It looks better on you." Nash says with a smirk.

We spend the rest of the night talking about us and our future together. Neither one of us slept last night. Nash makes us coffee with espresso. I observe him.

"I was able to learn how you like your coffee. I even took the machine with me."

"I don't know what to say." I lean into him, giving Nash a kiss on his cheek.

I don't know how in a matter of moments; it is like nothing has changed between us. I feel like I am whole again. I went from thinking I knew everything to realizing I only know how I feel right now. That feeling is peace. I am finally at peace with myself.

I admire Nash's face. "I love you so much."

"I know. We literally made it through hell."

I can't disagree. Even after all of that, it made us stronger.

I text Holden to let him know I am at Nash's. I know he will worry where I am if I don't tell him. Nash and I go to pick up Maverick from my apartment. We spend the rest of the day playing at the beach. I take in all the moments. I take photos of the three of us. I take one of Nash and Maverick with the ocean in the background. I know I will frame that one for my office.

After a few hours, we go back to Nash's apartment. Maverick curls up on the couch to take a nap. I follow Nash to his balcony. His view is almost as nice as mine. I place my head on his shoulder as we watch the waves crash on the shore. It seems to be one of our favorite things to do.

I may not know where life will take me next. I do know I am completely in love with my life right now. I am trying to focus on the right nows in life. Nash and I learned a valuable lesson. Life is way too short to take it for granted. I will savor every moment I have with the people that love me the most.